W9-BLL-077

The
TROUBLE
with GOOD
IDEAS

The TROUBLE with GOOD IDEAS

A M A N D A P A N I T C H

Roaring Brook Press
New York

Text copyright © 2021 by Amanda Panitch
Published by Roaring Brook Press
Roaring Brook Press is a division of Holtzbrinck Publishing Holdings
Limited Partnership
120 Broadway, New York, NY 10271

mackids.com

Library of Congress Cataloging-in-Publication Data is available.

ISBN: 978-1-250-24510-6

Our books may be purchased in bulk for promotional, educational, or
business use. Please contact your local bookseller or the Macmillan
Corporate and Premium Sales Department at (800) 221-7945 ext. 5442 or
by email at MacmillanSpecialMarkets@macmillan.com.

First edition, 2021
Book design by Cassie Gonzales
Printed in the United States of America by Bang Printing,
Brainerd, Minnesota

1   3   5   7   9   10   8   6   4   2

To all the Nevins, Gurneys, Moores, and
Panitches with whom I shared so many wonderful
Saturday afternoons at Zaide's.

CHAPTER ONE

AS FAR AS FAMILY INHERITANCES go, I got a bad deal. Like, my friend Julie's family has this beautiful ring that was originally her great-grandmother's and got passed down through the generations to the oldest daughter in each one. When she turns eighteen, she'll get to wear the ring, which, by the way, has an actual giant diamond in it.

Me? I got a nose.

Not, like, a nose cut off my great-grandmother's face and passed down in a box. I'd throw that straight in the garbage, thank you very much. I mean the nose on my face. Everybody on my mom's side of the family, as far back as pictures go, has the exact same nose. Long, with a bump in the middle and a little hook at the end. And really, really big.

I was staring straight at a mirror version of that nose right now over the chessboard. Just the nose, though, not the rest of the face. Not unless I'd aged eighty years and turned into a man in the last few minutes, which was unlikely. I think I would've felt that.

"Leah Roslyn?" Zaide asked. He'd just made his move, pushing his pawn forward a square, so it was my turn.

"I'm thinking," I said, which was true, even if it wasn't about the game.

Zaide shifted back in his seat. "Take all the time you need." He was missing most of his teeth, and he refused to wear dentures, so all his words came out with a lisp. Combined with the Yiddish accent he'd brought with him from Poland a million years ago, he could be hard to understand. But I was used to it. I could understand whatever he said.

Zaide is the Yiddish word for *grandfather*, but my zaide is actually my great-grandfather—aka my mom's grandfather. It's pronounced like *ZAY-dee*, which you wouldn't expect from its spelling. My family and I spent every Saturday afternoon at Zaide's house and had for as long as I could remember. Now we spent other days here, too, since we'd moved here to live closer to him. Like, much closer to him. As in down the street.

About a million years ago, my zaide bought an old telephone company building because it was a lot cheaper than a real house, and then he redid the inside all by himself, so that it had rugs and wallpaper and actual separate rooms. The walls were brick three feet thick, he said, and there were only two windows, one in the front of the house and one in the back. Half of the house consisted of the giant garage, which was musty and dark and still full of old, rusty phone company equipment. I could see it out the window from where I sat on the couch.

"Leah Roslyn?" Zaide prompted again.

"Still thinking," I said, though now I stared at the board. The pieces blurred before me. I was probably going to lose anyway. Zaide won at least 80 percent of our games. *I would never let you win*, he told me once. *That would be an insult to you.* Which made it way more exciting the first time I beat him, since I knew it was for real.

"Do you need a hint?" he asked. Just because he didn't let me win didn't mean he didn't help me. He had over eighty years of life experience on me, after all. So it was only fair.

I'd never gotten made fun of for our nose before we

moved here. The other day, I was at chorus rehearsal, and Emma Paglino, who is tiny and adorable with a pert nose like a pug's, stood in front of me and looked hard at my face. She said, "Oh! So it's true that Jewish people all have noses shaped like sixes."

It's probably important to note that, at my new school, I'm the only Jewish kid in all the sixth grade. This was not the case at my old school, which was a Jewish school, which meant we were *all* Jewish. And no, Emma Paglino, we did not all have noses shaped like sixes. I didn't say that, though. My cheeks just got really hot, and I pretended not to hear her, and then the teacher called my row, so I got to run away to the stage.

"Zaide," I said. "If you could change anything about yourself, what would it be?"

Zaide tilted his head, considering. That was another thing I liked about Zaide: He always took me seriously. Sometimes I asked my parents questions like this, and they just rolled their eyes, all like, *We have far more important things to do than listen to our one and only child, like muttering at our phones and complaining that our coffees are cold.* "I don't think I would change anything," he said. "Yes, I have had a hard life sometimes, but look at where it took me."

By that, he meant me and my family and my cousins, all here at his house. That was heartfelt and all, but it didn't answer my *real* question. "What about how you look?" I prompted.

He didn't stop to think this time, only smiled. It wasn't the prettiest smile, considering that there were barely any teeth and the ones that were left were all yellow, but it was pretty to me. "What would I change? This beautiful smile?"

I couldn't help but giggle. Only a little, though.

"This glowing skin?" Zaide ran a hand over one of his many deep, deep wrinkles. "This strong back?" He stretched a little to show off his hunch. "This glorious head of hair?" The light shone off his bald head.

Okay, this time I giggled kind of a lot.

I glanced down at the board, avoiding his eyes. I wanted a hint now, but I didn't really want to ask for one and make it obvious how much I didn't know. So I moved my queen across the board, snagging one of his knights.

"Leah, what are you talking about?" My cousin Matty looked up from her phone. I'd thought she wasn't paying attention to me, but apparently, she'd been listening this whole time from over where she sat on the cozy armchair. "Zaide doesn't need to change anything about himself."

I bristled at her know-it-all tone. She was only a year older than me, but she thought that one measly year made her, like, an entire adult. "I didn't say he did. Anyway, I'm focusing on the game."

I turned back to the board just in time for Zaide to nab my queen with his bishop. "Checkmate."

Argh. I searched the board, but he was right. My king was trapped, nowhere he could go to escape or, at least, hide from all the other chess pieces making comments about his nose.

Maybe that was me projecting a little.

"Good game," Zaide said, reaching over the board to shake my hand. I shook and said it back. He stood slowly, looking toward the kitchen. "I'm going to see what your parents are doing." His eyes traveled over to Jed, Matty's brother and my other cousin. "Jedidiah David."

Jed sat up from where he was lying on the floor. Yes, he was just lying on the floor for no reason. He was the oldest of us, but he still did things like that. "What?"

"We'll work on your math later," Zaide said. "No more Cs."

Jed's sticky-out ears flushed red. "Okay."

Zaide headed back to the kitchen, leaving me alone with Matty and Jed. As soon as Zaide disappeared into the other room, Matty set her phone down on the table and turned her eyes on me. "Leah, what were you getting at earlier? Do *you* want to change something about *your*self?"

I bristled again, this time because I hated how right she was and because she was going to make me say it. "Seriously? You have to ask me that?"

Jed said, his ears still pink, "I have no idea what you're talking about, either."

With a grand flourish, I pointed right at my nose.

Jed blinked. Matty blinked.

"My *nose*," I said.

Matty rolled her eyes. "Your nose is fine."

My nose is not fine. It's a villain's nose, which makes it not-fine by definition. Every time you see a character with a nose like mine—big and bumpy, with a hook at the end—they're evil. The Wicked Witch of the West. Professor Snape in Harry Potter. Jafar, Cinderella's wicked stepmother, Mother Gothel, and basically every other Disney villain. All of the princesses and heroines have sweet little button noses or baby ski slopes.

But Matty and Jed wouldn't understand. They don't

exactly have small noses, but they're not big, either, and they certainly don't have the hook at the end. Somehow they managed to avoid the terrible inheritance, though their dad has the nose. "When I turn eighteen, I'm going to get a nose job," I told them. I'd told my mom the same thing, but she hadn't taken me seriously. *It used to be that nose jobs were a big thing among Jewish girls, but not anymore*, she'd said. *Appreciate your differences! Have pride in them!*

But how was I supposed to appreciate and be proud when it was clearly a bad thing to have a nose like mine?

"You don't need a nose job, Leah," Matty said.

I would totally have answered her if Jed hadn't butted in. "I'm going to get a nose job, too," he said. "Except I'm going to have them make it bigger. And fatter."

"That's stupid," I said.

"You know what else is stupid?" he asked.

We said together, "Your face." It was a joke, but in this case it was actually true. My face *was* stupid, all because of my nose.

Then I got serious. "But really, it makes it so that I don't fit in, Matty."

She wrinkled her whole face at me. "Matilda." She'd started going by her full name a couple of months ago.

She said that Matty made her feel like a little kid. Like Matilda was so much more grown-up.

A crinkle came from the direction of the kitchen. Matty shot bolt upright. She had a superpower: She could tell what any food was based on how the wrapper sounded coming off. "Chocolate-covered caramels," she said breathlessly, jumping to her feet. "Hurry, before my dad stuffs them all in his face!"

She and Jed dashed off, feet loud on the carpet-covered concrete. I followed more slowly, plodding along, because Jed would make sure to save me some candy no matter what. This was what Saturday afternoons at Zaide's were made of: hanging out with Zaide and my cousins, playing some chess (usually losing), and eating lots of candy (to make me feel better after losing). I paused for a moment in the kitchen doorway, my nose forgotten, smiling at the sight of everybody shoveling caramels in their mouths. I never wanted it to end.

But if the universe listened to what we wanted, I'd have a small, cute, Disney-princess nose.

CHAPTER TWO

THE FOLLOWING SATURDAY, I WAS all revved up
for a chess rematch with Zaide—I was definitely going
to win this time, I was at least 20 percent sure—and
some more chocolate-covered caramels. I didn't even
wait for Mom and Dad to get ready with the food for
lunch. I just ran outside and down the block.

Zaide's beat-up black sedan, which Dad always said
looked like the car an FBI agent would drive, was the only
car in the driveway, which meant Matty and Jed weren't
here yet. Good, because they had no patience for chess.
I didn't knock on the door or ring the doorbell. I didn't
have to. The door was always unlocked.

Inside, Zaide's house smelled like steamed whitefish

and chicken soup, mostly because that's what he ate when we didn't bring him other things. As usual, the chessboard was set up and waiting: the knights with their lances in hand, the queens gazing imperiously over their territories. But nobody was in the living room, unless you counted the knights and queens as people. I continued on across the dining room toward the office, where Zaide kept a rolly chair and a desk stacked with papers. We were NOT ALLOWED TO TOUCH either one.

Zaide was standing beside the desk with the telephone receiver in his hand—he still had one of those super-old-fashioned ones with a curly cord and everything. It was clamped against his chest with one arm. The arm was shaking.

That was weird. "Hi, Zaide. Ready for a rematch?" I moved closer to him automatically, ready to give him our usual cheek kiss . . .

. . . only he lurched away, his backside hitting the desk and sending a stack of papers sliding to the floor. He extended the arm that wasn't holding the phone and pointed at me. "Who are you, and what are you doing in my house?" he demanded. His accent sounded thicker, his words harder to understand than usual.

He had to be joking. Only this wasn't a very funny joke.

I let out a brittle laugh. "It's me, Leah," I said. "Leah Roslyn. Your great-granddaughter." He just kept staring at me. "Come on, Zaide. This isn't funny."

The door creaked behind me, but I didn't turn around to see who'd come in. The four sets of footsteps stomping over the cement floor told me perfectly well who it was. Also, I didn't want to take my eyes off Zaide.

Matty and Jed stepped up beside me, flanking me on either side. "What's going on?" Matty whispered down at me.

Uncle Marvin approached Zaide cautiously. "Zaide, is everything okay?"

"He's joking around, and it's getting weird," I said. Everybody looked at me, probably because my voice had come out too loud. "Stop it, Zaide."

He blinked at me. I waited for the silent howl of his face to relax into its usual hollowed cheeks and maze of wrinkles. I waited.

I kept waiting.

"Zaide . . . ," Uncle Marvin said, but Zaide interrupted him, demanding, "Where is Ruthie? What did you people do with Ruthie?"

Ruthie? Oh. Ruthie had to be Ruth, aka Ruth Sarah Nevins, aka my great-grandmother, aka Zaide's wife. Bubbe Ruth had died when I was five. I didn't remember much of her besides a soft, warm lap and a kind laugh.

So why would he be asking for her?

"This isn't funny," I said again, weakly. Because I didn't really think he was joking, but I wasn't sure what else could be going on. Maybe there was something wrong with his eyesight? His hearing had been going for the past few years, meaning I had to talk louder and louder every time I saw him, so if he couldn't see or hear me, he might not know who I was.

But that didn't explain the Ruthie thing. It was a pretty big deal to forget that your wife was dead.

The door creaked open again behind us. That would be my parents. I wanted to turn to watch them as they hurried over, but I still didn't want to take my eyes off Zaide.

"What's going on?" I heard Mom say. She stopped short as she saw all of us. "Oh, Zaide." She said it as a sigh. "Kids, take this food and go into the kitchen."

I didn't want to go, but my insides were all shivery, and they wouldn't let me protest. As if moving on their own, my feet followed Matty and Jed into the kitchen. They didn't take a seat, just huddled in the corner near the candy basket, so I didn't sit, either. I set the food down on the table and joined them. None of us took any of the candy, even though that was usually the first place in the kitchen we beelined to.

"Hey, you guys," I said. "What do you—"

"Jed won his baseball game yesterday." Matty's voice came out sharp. She may have been talking about baseball, but what she was really saying was, *I don't want to talk about Zaide.*

Okay. That was fine. To be honest, I didn't want to talk about him, either. It was just that I didn't know how else to make the gut-punch feeling go away. "Mazel tov," I said to Jed.

Jed nudged Matty in the side with his elbow. They were both so much taller than me that if he tried the exact same gesture with me, he'd get my shoulder. "And guess who won her soccer tournament?"

Matty, I assumed. Otherwise that would be a pretty mean thing for Jed to do, and he was the exact opposite of mean. He was a giant marshmallow turned human. "Mazel tov," I said again. Matty and Jed played basically every sport that existed and probably some that didn't. (I was still convinced they'd made up squash.) They were on school teams and travel teams and would probably be on outer space teams if that ever became a thing.

Matty sniffed and tossed her hair over her shoulder. It was long and dark like mine, but hers fell in a straight sheet of shimmering silk. Even struggling for an hour with my straightener didn't make mine look like that. "I'm missing practice to be here today. And I'm the captain. The captain shouldn't be missing practices."

That was the thing about Saturday afternoons at Zaide's: They were mandatory. It was like going to school, where the only reason you couldn't go was if you were on the verge of death (at least, that was the case with my parents). I'd missed classmates' birthday parties and playdates all my life for our Saturday afternoons, but I didn't mind. Not usually, anyway. I'd almost always rather hang out with Matty and Jed.

"I'm sure your team will be fine without you," I told Matty, patting her on the shoulder, but that didn't seem to make her feel any better. "Do you guys want to go outside? We could throw rocks over the fence."

A buzzing sound. Matty fished her phone out of her pocket. Peeking at the screen over her shoulder, I saw her friends laughing as they kicked a soccer ball back and forth, bags of gear slung on their backs. They must have been heading to practice. Matty sighed down at her screen and let her thumbs fly.

I leaned my head in toward Jed. "How did your math test go?" I asked quietly.

Jed's face brightened. "Good! I got a B-plus." I let him fist-bump me as I told him congratulations. But then his face fell. I didn't know why he would look so sad after a good fist bump until he said, "It was all Zaide's help." He shook his head fast, like he was a dog coming in out of the rain, and when he finished, he looked a lot less sad. "I'm going to have some candy."

I bristled as he dove into the candy bowl—he obviously knew things weren't right, but he didn't want to think about it. With him distracted and Matty on her phone ignoring me, I pulled out my own phone like that was what I'd been planning to do anyway. I had actually missed some messages from a few hours ago in the group chat with my best friends from back home, Lexy and Julie. After we moved two hours away from them a few months ago, I'd seen them only a handful of times, at bar and bat mitzvahs or the occasional Sunday when we persuaded each set of parents to drive an hour to a mall that sat exactly between our two towns.

You aren't supposed to use your phone on Shabbat—the Jewish day of rest, aka Friday at sundown to Saturday at sundown—but my family is, let's say, *relaxed* about the rules. The same went for Lexy and Julie, who were currently at temple. They'd sent me a few selfies of themselves barricaded in the bathroom, then a picture of their deck of cards laid out on the floor. I felt a twinge in my chest. Sneaking out of morning services and playing cards with my friends in the bathroom was one of my favorite things to do. I sent, *Who won?*

The response came immediately from Lexy. *Naomi. But you probably would have won if you were here.*

Naomi? Who was Naomi? I squinted at the photos they'd sent me. They weren't actually selfies after all. Somebody else had taken them. Somebody else was behind the camera.

This *Naomi* person.

"Lssshhh gerrrr errrrtserrrd," Jed said before I could ask Lexy and Julie anything else. He had a mouth full of candy, but I was pretty sure he meant, *Let's go outside.* Matty nodded, still staring down at her phone.

The kitchen had a door that opened into the backyard, so we didn't have to walk through the house. Which was good because I didn't know if I could handle seeing Zaide looking at me like that again. Like I was some stranger. So when Jed opened the back door, I hurried outside as if it were a shimmering portal to another world.

Zaide's backyard was a backyard in the sense that it was an outdoor space in the back of the house. Remember, the house was once a telephone company, and telephone companies had no use for fields of green grass and wildflowers waving in the breeze. The backyard was pavement like the surface of a road, pitted and pockmarked with holes from years of snow and rain and maybe meteors or something. A tall chain-link fence circled it, separating it from the parking lot of a squat brown building, whose purpose we'd never been able to figure out, since nobody ever seemed to be over there.

Jed went up to the fence and wove his fingers into it like he was going to climb over. Matty stayed bowed over her phone. For some reason I didn't want to go back to mine, afraid I'd swipe away the lock screen and there would be a picture of Lexy, Julie, and Naomi having all the fun in the world while I was here being sad. I kicked at a piece of gravel, sending it skittering over the asphalt. It stopped right at the edge of the soup pot.

The soup pot wasn't a real soup pot, just like the

backyard wasn't a real backyard. The soup pot was what we called the biggest pothole behind the house. When we were little, we'd pick holly berries off the bushes out front and dandelion flowers and bits of sparkly rocks and dump them in the soup pot, then we'd mix it up and serve it in bowls to the grown-ups. They never ate it, which was super insulting to six-year-old Leah.

I thought about them all inside now, hovering around Zaide. "Do you think everything's okay in there?"

Neither one of them looked at me. Neither one of them said anything, either. Maybe they hadn't heard me. So I repeated the question, but louder.

"I heard you the first time," Matty said crossly.

Jed kicked the fence. It clanged against the ground. "You know what I think?" he asked. "I think we should've brought the candy bowl out with us."

"Those chocolate caramels were delicious," Matty said. "Maybe one of us should sneak in to get them. You're the smallest, Leah."

The last thing I wanted right now was candy. My stomach was churning. If I ate anything, I'd probably throw it up. "I don't want candy," I said. "Can't we talk about what's going on in there?" The two of them just looked around shiftily. I ground my teeth. Why wouldn't they just answer me?

All I wanted was for them to tell me that everything would be okay. That we'd always have our Saturday afternoons. No matter what was happening at school. No matter what wasn't happening at temple. That what just happened with Zaide wouldn't change everything.

The back door creaked open. Matty and Jed darted over, relief bright on their faces. My dad was standing there in the doorway, my aunt and uncle peering over each one of his shoulders. "Guys, we're going to head home," he said. He sounded exhausted, like it was one of those times I'd woken him up in the middle of the night because of a nightmare.

"Is Zaide okay?" Matty asked.

My dad hesitated a moment before answering. I might not have known what was going on, but I knew that hesitation never meant anything good. "Aunt Caroline is going to stay with Zaide for a bit," he said to her. Aunt Caroline was also known as my mom. "He's going to be okay. He just needs some time."

Some time. I hated it when adults said *give it time.* What that actually meant was they were hoping I'd forget about it and stop asking questions.

"Leah, we'll head around the side of the house," Dad said. I was tempted to push my way through the back door to see Zaide for myself, but the thought made my stomach hurt even more.

I turned to Matty and Jed. "Are you guys coming over for lunch?" I asked hopefully. Maybe they'd be more open to talking about all this when their stomachs were full. "We brought snacks."

My aunt and uncle stepped outside. Aunt Jessie checked her watch. "As tempting as that is, Lee, if we hurry we can still make it to Matilda's soccer practice."

"Yessss!" Matty pumped her fist in the air.

My shoulders slumped. Matty and Jed lived an hour away, so we went to different schools. Our once-a-week visit was the only time I really got to see them. I didn't want to wait till next Saturday to talk about all this with them. "But you're here anyway, so why not—"

"Let's go," Matty said quickly. She wasn't even listening to me. She gave me a quick one-armed squeeze, but I could tell her heart wasn't in it. "We'll hang out next week, Lee."

"I guess," I said, like I actually had a choice. "Bye, Jed. Bye, Matty."

Matty wrinkled her eyebrows at me. "Matilda."

"Right," I said, but I didn't actually say the word *Matilda*. "See you next week."

My dad and I walked past Zaide's squat brick house and then past all of our new neighbors, the gabled green Victorian and the two-story white colonial and the ranch house with the red roof. We didn't say a word the whole time.

CHAPTER THREE

MOM DIDN'T GET BACK FROM Zaide's until really late. She hadn't even texted me back when I asked if she was coming home for dinner. And when she finally dragged herself inside, her whole face was sagging like she'd aged ten years in this one day. I ran up to her, my own face a question, and she shook her head. "I can't talk about it right now, Leah."

Right. Give it some time. *Ugh.*

At least she told my dad the same thing before heading to bed. It's the worst when adults tell you they don't want to talk about something and then immediately go talk about it with another adult.

I didn't see her much on Sunday—she spent most of

the day alone with Zaide and then came home exhausted and not wanting to talk. She was still sleeping the next morning when I got up for school. She must have called in sick to work. She does something with taxes—I'm still not sure exactly what, even after years of career-day presentations at school.

Dad was already gone, which left me to make my own breakfast. *You are twelve years old and perfectly capable of pouring yourself a bowl of cereal*, Mom liked to say.

It was funny how I was all grown-up when she wanted me to do something and still a little kid when she didn't.

I zombied my way through the bus ride and most of the school day. I still felt out of place at Grover Cleveland Middle School, even though I'd been here since the beginning of the school year. I still sometimes went to say the *bracha*, the blessing, over my lunch the way we used to at Schechter, my old Jewish school.

I did that today, looking down at my turkey sandwich splayed out on the cafeteria table like I was about to dissect it. I opened my mouth in the shape of *Baruch atah Adonai*—after six years of Jewish school plus preschool, the words came as automatically to me as breath—then stopped myself. The girls at my table would look at me like I was weird. I made a fake cough like that was why

I'd opened my mouth in the first place, then stuffed some sandwich inside.

It might have made me look weird to bless the food, but it felt even weirder to eat food I hadn't blessed first. Like Hashem—God—might strike me down from above with a thunderbolt. Or just make me drop dead like the firstborn sons of the Egyptians in the story of Passover.

Deanna, Dallas, and Daisy would probably blink at me on the floor, all like, *Well, that's too bad*, then go back to talking among themselves like they were doing right now. I thought of them as the Three Ds because they were always together. Like triplets, even though they looked very different—Deanna was Black with a puff of dark hair; Dallas was pale with hair so blond it was almost white; and Daisy was somewhere in the middle with light brown skin and long black hair—I thought of them as almost identical somehow. They moved the same way, propping their chins on their hands and laughing with their heads tossed back, and they all sounded the same when they spoke.

They seemed to like me, in that they didn't make me leave their lunch table. We'd met because we all had to partner up for a science project. With me on the roster, our class had an even number of people, so they couldn't be a group of three the way they'd wanted. So Deanna and Dallas were partners, and I paired up with Daisy. I was new and had nobody to partner with, and she asked me quickly before she could get stuck with someone like Eugene Morton, who picked his nose and wiped it under his desk.

We got an A on the project, and I didn't know anyone else at Grover Cleveland Middle at the time, so I started sitting with them at lunch. It was better than sitting by myself, but I didn't speak much. Sometimes I laughed along at their jokes, though, like that would show them how much I belonged.

I tried not to think too hard about how I didn't. Belong, that is. We hadn't really had cliques at Schechter, and everybody mostly got along with everyone else, since the school was so small. And now I missed the feeling of knowing everyone, and of everyone knowing me. Grover Cleveland Middle was so big that it seemed like the only people who got to feel that way were in the popular crowd sitting at Isabella Lynch's table. I shot them a wistful look. They were all giggling, like they were just so happy at how wonderful their lives were.

Speaking of giggling, at my own table, Deanna was

winding up a story in that laughing tone that meant there was a punchline coming. I chewed fast and swallowed so that I'd have a food-free mouth in time. Nothing grosser than going to laugh and spraying wet crumbs all over the table.

". . . and Madison said, 'The thing we wanted was the blanket!'"

Dallas and Daisy burst out laughing. I laughed along, too, even though I'd missed most of the joke.

Deanna shot me a glance. "Sorry I didn't invite you, Leah," she said. "I was only allowed to invite a few people. And it was Friday night, so I figured you probably wouldn't be able to come anyway."

That *would* be the one thing she'd absorbed from me talking about my Jewish school at the beginning of the year. Somebody in class, hearing about the school I'd come from, asked if we had a Sabbath the way his family did on Sunday. I told him about Shabbat, the Jewish day of rest. If you're really religious, observing Shabbat means that you can't do anything considered work from sundown on Friday night to sundown on Saturday night. If that just meant homework or chores, I could get on board with that. But work traditionally also meant things like using electricity, pushing buttons, and driving. I like reading well enough, but that's basically all you can do on Shabbat, aside from going to temple for hours at night and in the morning.

But my family isn't that observant—back when I was at Schechter, I'd usually go to services on Friday night or Saturday morning, but not both. And we still drove and used electricity and stuff. Mom liked to say we tried to follow the spirit of Shabbat—relaxing more than usual and spending time with family. That's why our visits to Zaide were on Saturday afternoons.

I wondered what I hadn't been invited to. "No big deal," I told Deanna breezily, like I didn't care at all. My voice could have been rustling the fronds of a palm tree on a warm tropical beach. "But you know, my family isn't really strict about that."

Deanna exchanged a glance with the other two Ds. "Oh. We didn't realize."

What did that glance mean? Was it a glance like, *You guys were right—she's so weird*? Or a glance like, *This is awkward now*? Or, *How can she say that with a nose that size*?

They each had a small, snub nose. When they looked down at their shoes, there probably wasn't a blurry eyeful of nose in the way.

Now they were all glancing down at their trays or brown bags. *Oh no.* Was I supposed to have said something? I should say something to make this less uncomfortable. But what? What was I supposed to say?

I missed Schechter. And Lexy and Julie. Even if neither of them had a big nose like mine, I never felt out of place. I always knew what to say to them. I never had to explain what the Jewish holidays were or why I didn't eat pork. I scrambled for something to say.

"We don't eat bread on Passover," I blurted. *Wait. What? Why that?*

But it wasn't like I could take it back, so I just went all in. "Not bread, and not anything that's risen," I continued, waving my hands. "So no pasta or pizza or anything. For eight days. Basically all we can eat during Passover is potatoes and matzah. And matzah is terrible."

By the time I finished speaking, the only thing that stopped me from sliding under the table and hiding was how absolutely disgusting the cafeteria floor was. The Three Ds glanced at one another again. Dallas was the one who finally spoke. "That doesn't sound so bad!" she chirped. "I've had matzah before, and it was pretty good! Kind of like a saltine."

A shudder rippled through me. It wasn't even fake.

"All non-Jews say that," I told her. "Because you haven't been forced to eat it for every meal. It's basically cardboard."

One more glance. Maybe they had a secret language involving blinks and eye twitches, like Morse code. And they were saying, *Oh my God, why is she still talking about this?* I wanted to shrivel up like the empty potato chip bag next to my feet.

I pretended a little jump, like I'd felt my phone buzz in my pocket, and pulled it out. Maybe if I stared at it hard enough, they wouldn't notice how red I was.

No messages waited for me from Lexy and Julie since we'd texted last night about Julie's dad's terrible attempt at a kosher bacon substitute. Was it because of Naomi? *It's hard to be best friends when you don't ever get to see each other*, a part of my mind whispered. *Maybe they've replaced you. Probably they've replaced you. With Naomi, who has a tiny Disney-princess nose.*

I shoved those thoughts away. I had to send something, but I couldn't think of anything interesting to say. So I just sent our group chat a shouting emoji and typed, *Echo . . . echo . . . echo . . .* Then a sad face on the next line. Maybe that would guilt them into saving me from this awkwardness.

Only it didn't. I just stared at my phone, waiting for something to happen.

Something. Anything. The Three Ds' stares were burning a hole into my forehead.

I'd never been so happy to hear the bell ring. I hopped up, the uneaten half of my turkey sandwich forgotten. "See you in class!" I said like I hadn't just made a complete and total fool of myself. I fled before I could see them give one another those looks again.

I kept my head down the rest of the day, fleeing for the bus before I could say or do anything else embarrassing. Lexy and Julie didn't answer my echoes, which only made me feel more rotten.

My mood had lifted a bit by the time I got home. Maybe it wasn't really so bad what I'd said; it had just felt embarrassing at the time. Maybe the Three Ds wouldn't even remember it by tomorrow. Maybe Lexy's and Julie's phones were both dead. Or the principal had caught the girls using them and confiscated them until the end of the day. It had happened before. Principal Schwartz knew them both on a first-name basis.

I was in my head so much I didn't yell out that I was home the way I usually did. Not that it often mattered, since my parents were normally at work during the day.

I just liked getting to yell, and it warned any potential thieves or lurking ax murderers that they'd better start running.

Which was why it was so strange to hear my parents' voices coming from the kitchen. Then I remembered that my mom had stayed home today. But my dad should still be at work. I crept in the direction of the kitchen, not realizing I was trying to be quiet until I set my backpack gently on the floor instead of tossing it so that it landed with its usual satisfying thump.

"... worried it's getting dangerous," my dad was saying. That was strange. There wasn't much in our lives I would call dangerous. Dad even made fun of Mom for making us buy a big, blocky car because they were supposedly safer on the road than something flashier.

Mom sighed. Then she slurped. She was probably drinking tea. She liked to have tea when she was sick or really stressed out. Sometimes she'd make me some, too. I didn't like it, but I grimaced and drank it anyway. It made me feel grown-up. "I know," she said. "But what are we supposed to do? He won't listen to reason."

He?

A pause where I imagined Dad shaking his head. "It might be time to get a lawyer or something involved," he said. "The courts can appoint you or Marvin as a guardian, couldn't they? Surely there must be doctors who can make a judgment? We could call one of the assisted-living facilities on our list."

I blinked. Then blinked again. Something had short-circuited in my brain, and I couldn't stop blinking. Assisted-living facilities? That meant nursing homes, and I knew what nursing homes were thanks to hearing about them from my old friend Aaron from Schechter, whose great-grandmother was in one. The only old person we knew who could possibly use a nursing home was Zaide. And Zaide did *not* need to be in a nursing home. Just because he was old didn't mean he had to go live with all the other old people.

I pushed open the kitchen door, lifting my chin high into the air to make myself look taller and therefore more authoritative. "Zaide does not need to go to a nursing home," I proclaimed. In my imagination, this was where the conversation ended. Both my parents nodded vigorously, saying that of course I was right and how could they have thought otherwise.

In real life, it did not work out quite that way. Mom just sighed at me and looked even older. This close, I could see the gray saggy pouches beneath her eyes.

"Leah, number one, they're called assisted-living facilities now. A lot of them are very nice. Nicer than that telephone building, for sure. And two, this is not a conversation for you."

No matter how nice it was, it wouldn't be Zaide's home. I lifted my chin even higher. My parents could probably see up my nose now, no matter how hooked it was.

Ugh. Now I was thinking about my nose.

"Why not?" I asked. "He's my family, too."

"This is an adult conversation. Are you an adult?"

"My bat mitzvah is this year. Then I'll be an adult." At least in the Jewish religion.

"But you haven't had it yet, have you?"

I had not. I scowled at Mom and Dad. They knew that was a sore point, that they'd pulled me out of Schechter and moved me away the year before my bat mitzvah. It was too far to go to regular Hebrew school at the temple, and the only temple closer to our new house was an Orthodox one we didn't want to go to because they were *too* observant. Our "relaxed" rules in regard to Shabbat and keeping kosher wouldn't really fly. So I'd be preparing for my bat mitzvah in ten months by schlepping the two hours once a month to have a private lesson with the cantor and using recordings of him singing my haftarah and Torah portions to practice for when I'd get up in front of the congregation and do it myself.

And we'd moved here specifically to be close to Zaide. If my parents sent him away, all of that would have been for nothing. Nothing at all.

"I'll have my bat mitzvah in less than a year," I said. "It's not like I'll change that much in less than a year."

"We'll see," Mom said, but her words had an air of finality to them. Like instead of *We'll see*, she'd said *We're finished*. And Zaide *would* be going into a nursing home.

But Zaide was fine. Just because he'd had one bad day when he forgot something didn't mean he should be yanked from the home he'd lived in for a million years and shoved into a nursing home. If I had to go to a nursing home every time I forgot something, I'd get sent away after every single test at school.

Aaron had told me all about the nursing home his great-grandmother was in. It had been a terrible place, according to him. Everything was white, from the walls to the floors to the hospital beds, and it smelled like a mixture of mothballs and Lysol and vomit. Some of the old people were friendly and would smile at him, but others didn't do anything but stare vacantly at the wall or the television set. My parents could call it an assisted-living facility all they wanted, but you couldn't change what something was by changing its name. Otherwise all of my lunchtime turkey sandwiches would be pizza. They were just trying to cushion the blow. Make me feel better.

I couldn't picture Zaide in a nursing home. I backed out of the doorway, my heart racing. I'd go over to his house and warn him. Maybe we could run away together, two Jews in cowboy hats on the lam. I didn't know why I pictured cowboy hats, but it seemed right. "I'm going to Zaide's!" I hollered back to my parents. I slammed the front door behind me on my way out, hoping it made my parents' teeth rattle.

CHAPTER FOUR

WHEN I GOT TO HIS house, Zaide was up on the roof.

Not to jump or anything. He had to go up there sometimes to fiddle with the old-fashioned antenna that kept his TV working. Thanks to the telephone company that used to be there, a sturdy, bolted-down metal ladder ran up one of the brick walls, so it was easy enough to climb up (not that the ease had ever convinced my parents to let *me* do it). Really, just the fact that he could climb up on his roof at ninety-three years old was enough to demonstrate that he definitely didn't need a nursing home.

A few years ago, I'd thought it would be funny to yell, "Don't jump!" Except it had startled him, and he actually almost fell off the roof. So now whenever I saw him up there I just waited till he came down.

So I waited. But I had kind of a bad feeling in my stomach the whole time, like I really had to go to the bathroom. It hadn't been there before—it must have caught up with me once I stopped. Because what if he gave me that look again? What if he yelled at me like I was some stranger instead of his great-granddaughter?

My phone vibrated in my hand. I glanced down. Lexy had finally responded to my sad echoes in the group chat. *Sorry babe!! Naomi got us addicted to Clicksnail. I've been on that like all day. Love you lots tho*, with the floating hearts emoji. I knew what Clicksnail was; it basically let you send photos to one another covered up in filters and stuff, like half the other apps out there. But I wasn't allowed to put apps on my phone. My parents wouldn't let me. They said I was too young and it was too dangerous. Phone calls and messaging only, and I wasn't allowed to have a password on it, so that they could look at it anytime. They hadn't ever done it, because they trusted me, but I knew that they could. Maybe they'd make an exception for Clicksnail. If Lexy and Julie were on it, surely it couldn't be dangerous.

Suddenly the ladder clanged. Zaide was climbing

down. He didn't see me until he stepped onto the ground, and then his face broke into a huge smile. Even with his small amount of yellow teeth, it was the most beautiful smile I'd ever seen. "If it isn't Leah Roslyn," he said.

It's an Ashkenazi Jewish tradition not to name a baby after a relative unless the relative is already dead. Apparently, death might get confused or whatever and take the baby instead of the older relative, which I think says more about how stupid death is than anything else. Also, if I were an old person, I'd sneak into all the hospitals and write my name on all the birth certificates. Death would never find me then!

Anyway, I was named for my mom's mom, Zaide's daughter, who died before I was born. Her name was Roslyn. Sometimes he says she lives on in me.

I waited until we got inside and Zaide poured himself a steaming cup of tea. (What is it with adults and tea?) I shifted in the kitchen chair, feeling the stuffing poke my behind from where it stuck out of the tear in the seat. I wanted to fold my hands on the tabletop in front of me, but the table was sticky and gross. "Zaide, I have something important to tell you," I said, then stopped.

My eyes traveled to the calendar on the wall, which

changed every month to a different picture of me and/ or Matty and/or Jed throughout the years. The current picture was of me and Matty and Jed as little kids from some Saturday a long time ago, our faces scrunched up in hysterical laughter over a caricature an older second cousin had drawn of us.

A lump rose in my throat as I continued. "I heard Mom and Dad talk about taking you to a nursing home. We have to show them that you don't need it."

Zaide was quiet for a moment. Then he said, "This isn't for you to worry about, Leah Roslyn."

Despite his words, a tendril of relief twined its way through me at the sound of my name again. See, Mom and Dad? Everything was fine. He knew exactly who I was. "I think it is, though," I told him. "We should make a plan together. A game plan. Like in chess. We know what the king and queen are planning on doing, so we need to set up our defenses, right?"

Zaide took a sip of his tea, even though it still had to be way too hot. His lips must have been burned. When he put the cup down, his face showed no expression. "Leah Roslyn, do you know the story of the Golem of Prague?"

This really was not the time to be changing the

subject. But once Zaide got something in his mind, you just had to let him talk it out. "It sounds a little familiar," I said. Maybe one of my teachers had said something about it. There were a lot of things I didn't remember from school.

"It was the sixteenth century, in Prague, in what is now the Czech Republic," he said. Which was in Europe. I had to bite my lip not to be like, *Duh, I know where Prague is*. "In Prague in the sixteenth century, our people were under attack."

Again, I had to bite my lip. In all the stories from the old days, we Jews were always under attack, always being exiled or murdered or burned. Some kids grew up with family stories about being related to royalty or farming on the prairie. I grew up with stories about how my ancestors hid in attics so that they wouldn't die, and *By the way, Leah Roslyn, one day you might have to do the same because the world is never truly a safe place for us*. My friends and I used to talk about the non-Jews we knew who could hide us if the day ever came.

"Jews were forced to live in the poor, crowded ghetto, where the streets crawled not only with sickness but horror. Men would sweep the streets and terrorize them—even the women and the elderly—with no one to protect them," Zaide continued. "One day, the rabbi Judah Loew ben Bezalel grew tired of it all, and he made a plan. He gathered a pile of clay from the banks of the local river, he shaped it into a person, and he recited prayer after prayer. At the end, he pushed a paper inscribed with the *shem*—the true name of God—into the clay figure's mouth.

"And its eyes opened."

Zaide clearly meant this to be a shocking moment. I wasn't especially shocked, but I made an appropriately shocked-sounding gasp.

Pleased, he went on. "The rabbi called his creation a golem. At first, the golem protected the Jews of Prague from the angry mobs. It threw itself in front of weapons because its clay flesh could not bleed, and it carried people to safety on its back, running with inhuman speed." Zaide's face darkened. "But it could not last forever. The golem ... it ..." He trailed off into silence. His throat worked, his Adam's apple going up and down. It was like he was thinking of a way to say something he didn't want to say.

When he finally spoke again, it was with an effort. "The people could not all be saved. Eventually the piece of paper with the *shem* ... was torn from the golem's mouth, and the golem crumbled into dust." Zaide paused. "They had to save themselves."

I realized I was sitting on the edge of my seat. "And then what?"

Zaide steepled his fingers before him. "The rabbi gathered the broken bits of the golem and the scrap of paper and stowed it in the attic of the synagogue. Through the years, it passed through many different hands: visiting rabbis, traders, thieves." He raised his eyebrows. "By the 1900s, people thought it was lost. Until a young boy discovered a mysterious packet in the cellar of a synagogue in Knyszyn, Poland."

I gave an uncertain laugh. I knew Zaide was from Knyszyn. He had fled Poland around the time of the Holocaust, when more than six million Jews and millions of other "undesirables" were murdered by the Nazis and their supporters because they were Jewish or Romani or even gay. He had made it out in time with his parents and two older brothers. Most of his cousins hadn't. His own Matties and Jeds.

"It was a dangerous time to be a Jew in Poland then," he said, his eyes misty. "My parents were talking about fleeing, but we didn't know where to go. Most countries wouldn't take us. So I formed a plan of my own."

He described how he'd wet the clay he'd found in the packet and combined it with the dirt from his own village, forming it into the shape of a person. Stuffed the *shem* in its mouth. "And it opened its eyes," Zaide continued. I raised an eyebrow skeptically. "I had big plans. Oh, I had big plans. I was going to use the golem to save our village from the Nazis, then save all the Jews in Poland. When the nearby villagers came to attack, the golem fought them off."

Zaide shook his head. I wanted to shake my head, too. Did he really think I would believe this? I wasn't a baby anymore. I no longer thought the tooth fairy swapped my teeth for money so that she could build a massive castle in the clouds out of tooth bricks. "I thought we would be safe. I let the golem's presence lull me into peace. Let me think we would be okay and we wouldn't have to leave." His face darkened, as if there was a storm passing behind his eyes. "But . . . those were deceiving thoughts." His Adam's apple did the same thing as before, like he couldn't get out what he wanted to say. "We . . . we barely made it out in time."

I waited for Zaide to continue, but he only settled back into his chair and took a sip of tea. "Is that it?"

He lowered the tea and looked at me calmly. "Leah

Roslyn, sometimes a person must fight their own battles."

Under the lisp and the Yiddish accent, what he was really saying was *Leah, stay out of it.* But I couldn't. It wasn't fair, just him going up against my parents. It should at least be two against two. How were you supposed to win if you were missing half your pieces? "But—"

He set his teacup down hard enough that a few drops of tea splashed over the rim and onto the table. That was why it was always sticky. "Your parents are probably looking for you. Don't make them worry."

My cheeks burned. That was him saying *Leah, go home.* Why couldn't people just say what they meant? "But I—"

He stood up abruptly. Conversation over. "I love you very much, Leah Roslyn. I love your parents very much, too."

Even with everything they were doing to him? I trailed after him as he walked slowly toward the door. He might walk slowly, but he didn't even need a cane or anything. My parents couldn't put him somewhere where they'd just stick him in a wheelchair and where Matty and Jed and I might not get to visit. He'd waste away.

Zaide bent over to open the door—he didn't even moan the way Dad did about his bad back.

Maybe *Dad* should be the one going to a nursing home.

Hands closed over my shoulders. "It's going to be all right," Zaide told me. "Thank you, Leah."

I swallowed hard. I had to swallow hard to get over the lump that had risen in there sometime in the last few seconds. "If you meant that, you'd let me help you," I told him, and I pulled away. I didn't glance over my shoulder as I left, not at all. I didn't care if he was looking at me.

CHAPTER FIVE

MOM AND DAD WERE WAITING for me when I dragged myself up the front steps and in through the front door, but I was *not* in the mood. "Excuse me," I said, trying to barrel past.

They didn't move. Mom took a deep breath. "Listen. Leah."

I crossed my arms over my chest and hugged them tight. "I told Zaide that you guys wanted to put him in a nursing home."

Mom and Dad sighed in unison. "Oh, Leah," Mom said wearily. "I wish you hadn't done that."

"Why not?" I said it like I was daring her. "If you're going to do it, you should own it."

"It's not that," Dad said. "Leah. We haven't made a decision yet. But if we did talk to Zaide about an assisted-living facility, it would be because it's for his own good. It's hard for him to be alone now, and it's only going to get harder."

If it was hard to be alone, well, I had a solution for that, and it barely took me any time to think of it. "I can move in with him then," I said. "It's right down the block, so it's not like I'd have to worry about changing schools. I'd even be able to catch the same bus!"

"Leah—"

"And he has that extra bedroom nobody even uses." I talked right over my mom. "So it's perfect! Then nothing has to change."

Mom shook her head. "What happens when he wakes up and he doesn't know who you are?" she asked. "Or—"

"That was once!" I interrupted. And really, the situation hadn't been entirely clear. Maybe he just hadn't been able to see me.

"It wasn't once, Leah. There was that time last week, and twice last month, and—"

"I don't remember any of those," I said loudly, anything to make her stop. My face was getting really hot, which meant it was getting really red. "He was fine today. I just got back from his house—his *home*—and he was totally *fine*."

"These things come and go," Dad said. "But they keep getting worse."

I stamped my foot. "We moved all the way here so that we'd be here with him and he wouldn't be alone. That's why I had to change schools and everything."

Mom sighed again. "I know, and I'm sorry. We didn't realize how bad it was until we actually got here and started seeing him every day."

"Fine," I said, throwing my hands up. "Then why can't he move in with us? We have an extra bedroom, too. It would be fun! Like a permanent sleepover."

Mom and Dad exchanged a glance. "We've talked about it," Mom said, and her voice was cautious, like she was trying not to disturb a sleeping bear. "But Zaide will require special care as he . . . as his condition progresses. And I'm telling you, Leah, these places we're looking at aren't nursing homes like you're thinking. They're almost like hotels, except that they have people there round-the-clock to help them and keep them safe. Which is something we can't offer at home. A full-time live-in nurse like that is *very* expensive."

"So the nurse doesn't have to come all the time—they can come sometimes," I argued. "And—"

My dad broke in. "Leah. This is getting emotional. Let's table this discussion for now."

Right. He might as well have said *give it time*.

"Whatever," I said. "Fine." Maybe they realized how upset I was right now, and I could use their guilt to my advantage. "I wanted to ask you—I know I'm not supposed to have apps on my phone, but can I get Clicksnail? Lexy and Julie are on it." My dad was already squinting at me in the way that meant no, so I hurried to speak before he could actually say it. "It's not dangerous. It's just sending photos back and forth. You can even add me on it so you can see the stories I post."

"We've discussed this, Leah," said Dad, and he didn't even have to say the *no*. It was there in his voice.

Hate burned through me right then, quick and fierce. It was like they were purposefully trying to destroy my life. They were making me lose Lexy and Julie to this stupid Naomi. They were trying to lock Zaide away when anybody could see he was fine. And without our Saturday afternoons at Zaide's house, I wouldn't just lose Zaide and all my skills at chess, I'd lose Matty and Jed to soccer and baseball and their cooler, older friends.

I'd already lost so much. I couldn't lose them, too.

I opened my mouth, then closed it. If I let myself say what I wanted to say, I'd get grounded till the earth froze over. So I stomped up the stairs and slammed my bedroom door behind me, just so my parents would know how mad I was.

The rest of the week flew by. I didn't say anything stupid to the Three Ds, because I didn't say much of anything at all. I laughed along with their jokes, whether or not they were funny, and they didn't roll their eyes at me or exchange any more of those glances. I tried to text Lexy and Julie at least once a day around lunch, something funny I thought of or asking them how they were doing. They'd text me back, but it didn't feel like our friendship before. I didn't know what was happening with them day to day anymore, and they didn't know what was happening with me. Probably because they were busy on Clicksnail with Naomi.

On Thursday, I wore a pink shirt and jeans to school the same day Isabella Lynch wore a pink shirt and jeans, and she stopped by my locker and flashed me a rare smile. "Hey! Twinsies!" I smiled but totally blanked on an acceptable response, so I stayed quiet. Better to be quiet than accidentally say something stupid and look like a loser in front of the most popular girl in the sixth grade.

By the time Saturday afternoon rolled around, I was determined to get Matty and Jed on my side. My insides thrummed impatiently as they greeted Zaide and answered the usual small-talk questions from my mom. ("How's school?" School was always "good" or "fine," Mom. That's a stupid question.) Finally, I was able to lead them from the kitchen, where the adults gathered, to the living room, where we clustered on the red velvet couch.

"You guys," I said, lowering my voice and leaning in. I had to tell them right away. And not just because I didn't want to give them the chance to ask me about school. "I heard my parents talking the other day. They're thinking about putting Zaide in a *nursing home*."

I waited for Jed and Matty to erupt. They might even be loud enough for the adults to hear and come running. *This is an outrage! How dare they! We'll fight to the last man—or girl!*

I kept waiting. They just looked calmly at me, not even raising their eyebrows with surprise. They knew.

Somehow they knew. I said through clenched teeth, "Who told you?"

"We overheard our parents talking about it the other day," Matty said. My clenched teeth relaxed. They'd found out just like me. "We would've told you, but it's not actually going to happen, so it's not a big deal."

She tossed her hair and smiled, like the situation was resolved. But Jed was still looking at me. "Seriously, Lee, don't worry," he said quietly. "They can't force Zaide to do anything he doesn't want to do."

He laid a comforting hand on my arm, and for a second, I let it sit. He was invested in this as much as I was, really. But then I pulled away because he wasn't being realistic. His hand fell to the floor. "Sure they can," I said hotly. "They were talking about getting themselves assigned as guardians or something so they could do *exactly* that."

"What can we do about it?" Matty said to me. I frowned because her words were combative, but . . . her voice wasn't. She sounded helpless.

And when I looked into her eyes, they were shiny.

First off, she needed a hug. So I gave her one. Then I leaned back and said words I knew she didn't want to hear. "Maybe nothing. But we have to try. And we can start by talking about it."

"I just don't want to talk about it," Matty said. "It's too hard."

"But you can't just pretend it isn't happening," I argued.

She stared at me. I stared back at her. We were like the opposing queens of a chess set, forever poised for battle.

Then Jed broke in. He was like a knight, leapfrogging over the pawns to surprise us. "Guys, let's go sneak into the garage."

Matty looked away. I let my breath out in a loud whoosh. "Okay. Fine." I'd let them off the hook for a little while longer. The garage was always worth a trip, the coolest part of an already cool house.

"We're going outside!" Jed shouted into the kitchen. Nobody said anything in response. Come to think of it, it was probably pretty awkward in there, what with Zaide being fully aware that the other four adults in the room were ganging up on him and wanting to send him to what was basically a hospital-jail. At least, it was awkward enough that none of the adults even thought to call back, *Why are you going outside when it's like thirty degrees out there?*

It was pretty chilly in the garage, too. The ceiling stretched two or three stories overhead, and the lights above hardly served to make a dent in the dense tangle of stuff, especially toward the back. We'd been sneaking out here probably once a month for years now, and we still hadn't been able to examine everything. Half the stuff was rusty old machines and detritus left behind by the telephone company, another half was old farm equipment Zaide and Bubbe Ruth had brought with them fifty years ago when they sold their chicken farm, and a third half was old things they'd accumulated in these past fifty years and couldn't bear to throw away. Yes, if you were counting, I did just list three halves. There was *that . . . much . . . stuff.*

Matty was convinced there was treasure hiding somewhere in the back. She had not yet succeeded in convincing me or Jed.

"Where should we start this time?" Matty asked, but she was already winding her way toward the back, her phone out to act as a flashlight. We'd checked out the front section a thousand times—mostly pieces of old furniture, an armchair with coils poking through the seat and a three-legged table among them—so we obediently followed her. Jed went next, pushing large pieces of equipment out of the way so that they wouldn't fall over and smash me.

Being in the back of the garage felt like being in a thicket, the three of us small beneath looming shadows of sharp, dangerous-looking things. Sometimes I was convinced the garage went on forever. I cast an eye around. Something big with blades that I didn't want to get too close to lurked on my left, so I moved toward the right. There rested an old chest of drawers with a fleur-de-lis pattern, so many chips of paint missing that it was mostly just bare wood now.

Jed and Matty were somewhere close ahead. Matty whooped. "Lee, there's a toilet back here!"

While they were fascinated by the toilet, I slid the top drawer open. A few books were strewn inside. I picked one up and turned it over. It was in either Hebrew or Yiddish; I didn't understand more than a few words in either, but I could read their common alphabet. This book was a copy of the book of Genesis, and from its tattered black cover and yellowed pages, it looked really old. I flipped through the opening pages, my eyes catching on the year the book was published. 1882! Really old was right. Even Zaide hadn't been alive back then. This must have belonged to his own mother and father . . . or even his grandparents.

Maybe there were more things in the drawers that Zaide had brought over from the old country, more little bits from his past. The next drawer held a collection of what looked like old electrician manuals, filled with diagrams of plugs and sockets and wires—which made sense, since Zaide had become an electrician after being a farmer. These manuals must have been what he used to study. The third one contained a tumble of costume jewelry and some scarves that smelled like mothballs. Maybe they'd belonged to my grandma or great-grandma. I smiled at the thought of Zaide playing dress-up with them. Those clip-on earrings would look great with his bald head.

In the bottom drawer rested an envelope—not a letter-size one, but one of the big ones that could fit a whole unfolded packet of paper. I picked it up. Something rustled inside, the sound my shoes made when I got back from the beach and dumped out all the sand.

That was odd. Why would Zaide have kept an envelope of sand lying around? Granted, an envelope of sand was probably more useful than all the broken machinery that hadn't been used in fifty years. He claimed he'd learned from the Great Depression never to throw anything away, because you never knew when you might need it. Mom and Dad said that Zaide was a hoarder.

The envelope was sealed shut, but it had probably been out here for fifty years—nobody would notice if I opened it. I couldn't even see Jed and Matty at this point. They'd been swallowed by the shadows in the back, but I figured they were okay as long as I didn't hear any screaming. I cracked the envelope open and peered inside.

My first thought had been correct: The envelope was full of dirt. I tipped the envelope from side to side, trying to see if maybe there was something hidden beneath the dirt, but . . . well, it was just dirt.

Wait. I tipped the envelope a little bit farther to the side. I couldn't explain why, but my heart started beating fast. Like it knew something big was coming. A hidden birth certificate that proved I was actually the daughter of a famous movie star who'd had to send me into hiding so I wouldn't be warped by her fame. Or something. Not that I'd ever thought about that as a possibility before.

It was not a secret birth certificate, movie star–related or otherwise. It was a scrap of paper as yellowed as the pages of Zaide's old books. When I reached into the envelope to pull it out, a corner of it crumbled into the dirt.

Upon the scrap of paper were written Hebrew letters. I sounded them out slowly from right to left. A jolt ran through me as I closed my lips over the last syllable. Was that . . . ? It was . . . ?

Zaide's words from several days ago ran through my head. *At the end, he pushed a paper inscribed with the* shem—*the true name of God—into the clay figure's mouth.* That would mean . . . that this was . . . I squinted into the envelope, like the dirt might suddenly form itself into a person and wave hello.

It did not.

I shook my head at myself, sticking the piece of paper back inside the envelope. Nobody was supposed to know the true name of God—it was lost to time. What I was thinking was crazy. Golems were not a real thing, no matter what Zaide said. If he'd been telling that story as fact, maybe it *was* time for him to go into a nursing home. I snorted, half in laughter and half in horror at myself for making a joke like that, even if it was only in my own head.

Though . . . my parents' words raced by after Zaide's.

It's hard for him to be alone now, and it's only going to get harder. If golems *were* real, maybe one could live with Zaide and keep him company. Make sure he was okay.

If. That was the key word.

"Leah!" Matty's voice had a weird echo. "Look what we found!"

I stood on my tiptoes to see over the ancient refrigerator in front of me—half the size of the one we had at home—and could just barely glimpse Matty and Jed making duck faces at me in the light from her phone. They must have found an old hat rack, as each of them wore an impressively hideous cap. Matty's was an old-fashioned fedora with a lime-green plaid pattern, while Jed's was wide brimmed and bright red, with a feathered plume sticking straight out of it. I couldn't hold back a laugh as I pictured Zaide wearing either one.

"Come on!" Matty said. "There are lots more here. Leah, I think you should wear this one to school. *That* will make you popular." She waved a neon pink wicker monstrosity at me.

"I'm coming," I said, stepping forward. And then stopped. Without thinking too hard about what I was doing, I slid the envelope into my waistband and covered it with my shirt.

CHAPTER SIX

THAT NIGHT, I SHOVED MY face into my pillow and made myself go to sleep. The night after, I thought about the envelope I'd hidden away in my desk before I dismissed the thoughts as ridiculous. The night after that, those thoughts lasted another couple of minutes before I mentally told them, *Go away, because you are being absurd.* And the night after that, when my parents still refused to talk to me about Zaide, that voice in my head was a little bit less convincing.

On Friday night, I lay in bed in my pajamas and stared at the ceiling. I couldn't stop thinking about it all. The envelope of dirt and the ancient *shem*. Which was ridiculous. Magic wasn't real. Golems weren't real.

But . . . *what if*?

No. *You're not a little kid anymore, Leah. You know it's not real.*

And yet . . . *what if it is*?

I threw the covers off myself. I was getting warm anyway. Like my body was running along with my mind.

If golems were real, I could make one and have it take care of Zaide so that he wouldn't have to go to the nursing home, and I could keep my Saturday afternoons with him and Matty and Jed, and Matty wouldn't disappear with her cool soccer friends, and Jed wouldn't fail math. If Mom and Dad noticed something was off, all I'd have to do is remove the *shem* from the golem's mouth, and it would crumble back into a pile of dirt. Or maybe they'd even be all for this plan. It couldn't hurt to try, right? Nobody would ever have to know if I failed.

But where could I mix this? It wasn't like I could head down to the kitchen and pull out a mixing bowl, collect a scoopful of dirt from the yard, and roll it out on the kitchen counter like bread dough. One, my parents might wake up and ask me what I was doing, and I would have no idea what to say to them. Two, even if they didn't wake up, I'd make a huge mess and have to deal with cleaning it up. That crossed anywhere else inside off my list. So I'd have to go outside. I'd need to find somewhere with a big enough bowl to mix a bunch of dirt without making a—

The soup pot. The soup pot! It was embarrassing that it had taken me this long to think of it. Matty, Jed, and I had mixed enough "soup" in that giant pothole that some extra dirt wouldn't even be noticed.

I swung my legs off the side of the bed. If I tried to make a golem right now while nobody was around to watch, I couldn't be embarrassed when it failed. If Matty and Jed didn't know about it, they couldn't say I was being babyish for believing in magic. Even though I didn't believe in magic. But still.

Maybe I did believe, a little bit. Otherwise I wouldn't keep asking myself *what if*.

My school clothes from today were still draped over the back of my desk chair: black leggings, a green plaid skirt that looked almost like a school uniform, a white shirt with ruffled sleeves. It was fancier than the type of thing I usually wore, but I'd seen the mannequin wearing the outfit at the store. It had looked *exactly* like something Isabella Lynch would wear, and so I begged my mom to get it for me, even though it wasn't on the clearance rack and she usually liked shopping only on the clearance rack. I hesitated, then put on a T-shirt and jeans. I was going to be mixing a bunch of dirt together. I didn't want to get my Isabella Lynch outfit dirty, even if it was going in the wash soon. Carefully, I pulled the envelope out of the desk drawer.

Down the stairs, my sock feet slipping smoothly over the wooden surface. I knew enough to avoid the center of the two steps in the middle, where they creaked. Downstairs, the foyer was dim and gloomy, moonlight filtering in from outside so that everything wasn't just black.

I glanced into the living room to the right. Nobody was curled up and snoring on the comfy green couch. To the left. Nobody was enjoying a late-night snack at the dining room table, though my own face stared back eerily from the mirrored curio cabinet, pale as a moon. I stared myself in the eye and took a deep breath. Then I slipped out the front door and into the night.

Our block was not actually that spooky, even this late. Streetlights cast warm pools of light on the half-dead lawns and sidewalks so that I didn't have to walk in the dark until Zaide's backyard. A neighbor I didn't recognize was out, wearing a heavy coat over what looked like pajamas, yanking a stubborn beagle along on a leash. She called him a bad word as he stopped to sniff every pile of leaves and blade of grass. "God *bleep* it, go to the *bleeping* bathroom already."

The dog was so cute. I made a mental note to ask Mom for a dog.

When I got to Zaide's house, I stole into the side yard. I didn't have to worry about waking him up, not like my footsteps were going to be loud enough to wake a mouse through three-foot-thick brick walls. He was going a little deaf in his old age. It actually made his house better because he'd had to install Christmas lights that blinked and flashed whenever his house phone rang so that he wouldn't miss a call.

I made another mental note to ask Zaide how he expected to hear the person on the other end if he couldn't even hear the phone ringing.

Thinking about that kept me busy as I crept toward the soup pot. It wasn't visible from the front of the house, but it was lit up by the lights of the parking lot behind the fence.

I crouched on the pavement next to the soup pot and set the envelope down beside me. There wasn't that much dirt in the envelope, so I'd have to collect dirt from Zaide's yard to mix with it. I still wouldn't have enough to make a person-size sculpture, but Zaide hadn't said anything about making his golem life-size. Besides, nothing was going to happen, and I was going to end up feeling stupid.

And yet, *what if* . . .

It was fortunately misty enough out that the dirt was good and sticky and clumpy. I hauled a few armfuls from Zaide's yard to the soup pot; if he noticed the hole the next day, he'd blame it on squirrels or moles. Not that he would notice. He took pride in his wild lawn, in the bright yellow spots of dandelions and wiry patches of wild onion everybody else on the street tried to get rid of. *The weeds are just living their lives. Who am I to interfere?* he'd say, and then he'd pick a piece of wild onion and chew on it with his few remaining teeth, and his breath would smell gross when he kissed me goodbye.

The soup pot was now nearly full. I carefully lifted the envelope and poured its dirt inside, making sure to grab the *shem* before it could flutter away on the breeze. I gently tucked the paper into my pocket, where it would be safe while I sculpted its new residence.

Now. First things first. How was I supposed to go about making a golem?

I probably should have googled this or something.

My hands moved by instinct. Sure, I could make it

look like the typical lumpy clay brute, but I didn't want Zaide to have a heart attack if he found it sitting in the kitchen. Instead, while I worked, I thought about how I was the only person Zaide could really trust, about how I was the only one who didn't want to send him away. I could make Zaide a golem that was just like me. But maybe even a little bit better.

I mostly liked the way I looked. I imagined on the golem my wild brown hair, my cheeks that were so rosy Lexy used to say I didn't even need makeup, and my brown eyes that glowed gold in the right light. But of course I gave it a normal nose.

My mind wandered as my fingers worked the clay. If I were a golem, what else would I want?

To fit in and be popular at school. To sit at Isabella Lynch's lunch table and know instinctively when to laugh. To have everybody know me and like me and want to *be* like me.

To fit in with the world, too. To get to tell exciting family stories about being descended from a duke in England or a chief in Nigeria and not have to give the usual speech about how so much Jewish history in Europe was destroyed during the Holocaust that I didn't know exactly where I'd come from, but probably from peasants hiding from people who wanted to kill them throughout the centuries. To feel more normal and not have to worry about who'd hide me in their attic if the time ever came here.

My fingers dug and smoothed, pinched and poked. I'd want to know exactly how to understand people, to know what they were thinking, to know what was coming. Like in chess. I'd be able to win more than just 20 percent of the time if I knew how to manipulate the board. Or if I knew what was going on in Zaide's mind, what he was seeing.

Or Matty's and Jed's minds, a little part of me whispered. I frowned, punching the clay harder with frustration. They couldn't ignore the problem with Zaide forever. I'd want to know exactly how to make them talk and how to make them listen.

I had lots of ideas. But in reality, I was no sculptor, and what I was working with wasn't exactly fine clay—it had too many pebbles in it. In the end, what I was left with looked like a pile of dirt with some lumps. I just had to hope that she'd absorbed my intentions. As long as you had good intentions, that was what mattered, right?

"Open wide," I murmured. I'd given her a hole for a

mouth, so she didn't have to actually open anything, and also she was an inanimate lump of dirt, so she *couldn't* actually open anything. But whatever. I folded the *shem* as small as I could without tearing the fragile paper and shoved it into my lumpy golem's mouth hole. I wasn't sure if I was supposed to say anything or if the original ancient rabbi's incantations over this dirt and paper would hold.

"Okay," I said, waving my hands over it in a mystical sort of way. Then I felt silly, so I stopped. "Here we go. Come to life, please. Um. *Baruch atah Adonai, Eloheinu melech ha'olam, hamotzi lechem min ha'aretz. Amen.*" That was the blessing said over bread, but I didn't know what else to say. Bread rose the way I wanted this golem to rise, so maybe they were similar enough?

I sat back on my heels and waited. And waited.

And waited.

I'd been waiting about forever minutes when I started feeling even sillier than when I'd waved my arms around over the soup pot. Of course this wasn't going to work. What had I been thinking? "Stupid," I said aloud, rising to my feet. My knees hurt from where the gravel stuck to them, but I deserved it. Hopefully, my parents hadn't noticed I was gone. I had no idea how I'd explain my absence to them.

As I was rounding the corner back to Zaide's front yard, a rustling noise rose behind me. I stopped in my tracks. Even my heart stopped for a second.

Was that . . . ?

But then a bird burst free from the branches above. My heart jump-started and raced along with my feet as I hustled toward my house. "Stupid, stupid," I mumbled to myself.

When I heard another rustle behind me, I didn't even bother looking back.

CHAPTER SEVEN

I SOMEHOW FELT EVEN STUPIDER Saturday morning. Maybe it was the bright light streaming through my blue checkered curtains. In the dark and the haze of almost sleep, anything seems possible: That looming shadowy form on the other side of the room is a monster; that wrinkle in the shower curtain means there's a murderer hiding behind it. Then you turn on the light, and the monster is only a pile of clothes on your chair, and the shower curtain IS ACTUALLY HIDING A MURDERER! WATCH OUT!

Just kidding. There is not a murderer hiding in your shower.

Probably.

Downstairs, Dad was frying eggs in the kitchen. I padded in and sat at the table, my cheeks creaking in a yawn. "Sleep well?" he asked me.

Good. He suspected nothing. "Okay," I said.

After breakfast I read some of my fantasy book, and then it was already time to head over to Zaide's. I put on my green skirt / black leggings / white flouncy shirt combo because I wanted Matty to see how fashionable I was, and waited for Mom and Dad.

We got there before Matty and Jed. Mom and Dad went into the kitchen to put the chicken salad they'd brought over for lunch in the fridge while I said hello to Zaide. His papery lips brushed against my forehead. "Leah Roslyn," he said. It felt good to hear my name come out of his mouth. I had to fight the urge to look victoriously over at Mom and Dad. *See? He knows us; he knows exactly where he is.* "How are you today?"

I hesitated for a moment, then decided to answer honestly. "Not great, but not terrible."

He laughed. "Your honesty is refreshing, my dear." The laugh dropped away. "I have been thinking about what you said at our chess game a couple weeks ago."

I looked around to make sure Mom and Dad were too

far away to eavesdrop. I was sick of hearing them tell me I should take pride in my nose.

Zaide stared straight into my eyes. I squirmed a little in my seat because something about the weight of his gaze made me feel like he was staring into my very soul. "You seemed to think there was something I should be changing about myself in order to be happy."

That was exactly *not* what I'd said. "I think you're perfect just the way you are," I assured him. *Unlike my parents*, I thought, but didn't add.

His eyes wrinkled extra as he smiled. Which was saying something, since the rest of his face was basically one giant wrinkle. "Leah Roslyn, I have a secret to tell you."

I loved secrets! I leaned in to hear it.

"Sometimes I think it would be nice to have more teeth or fewer wrinkles," he said.

I leaned back. That was a disappointing secret, but you couldn't tell someone that, so I just nodded in what I hoped was a sympathetic way.

"I miss the feeling of people not immediately assuming I am weak and doddering and deaf because I am so old and toothless," Zaide went on. He was getting pretty deaf, but that was beside the point.

"You know, there's plastic surgery for that," I told him. Like how I was going to get a nose job someday. He might not know that he could get fake teeth or some of those wrinkles smoothed out.

He shook his head. "Not interested," he said. "I know changing my appearance would not change me on the inside. I would still be old. I have still lived all of these years, and I am proud of them. Look at what I've made!"

He might have been talking about the old telephone company building, but I chose to believe he was talking about me.

"Zaide?" Mom asked, stepping over. "What's going on?"

Zaide winked at me. I tried to wink back, but I think it was actually just a blink. "Nothing."

While Mom and Dad talked to Zaide about boring adult things—they didn't talk about the "assisted-living facility," which was surprising to me because if I were Zaide, that would be all I could talk about with them—I wandered out into the living space. A corner of the rug was peeling up, revealing the gray concrete beneath. I sighed. It was boring in here without my cousins, and something was simmering inside me. A little bit of annoyance at Zaide. He'd clearly been talking about me and my nose, but he didn't understand the situation.

People *did* treat me worse and think of me differently because of my nose, so obviously getting it taken care of would change that. No matter what he said.

"I'm going outside to wait for Matty and Jed!" I hollered back toward the kitchen. Nobody answered, which I took as a *fine*.

It was still chilly outside for March, but I was fine with my coat on. I paced back and forth across the front yard. I couldn't believe I'd been here last night in the light of the moon. What had I been thinking? I snorted a laugh at myself.

"Hello? Is someone there?" The voice was young and clear as a bell . . . and it was coming from around the side of the house.

I stiffened. There shouldn't be anyone over there. Matty and Jed and I had spent our entire childhood trying to figure out a way through that fence; it wasn't fair if some other kid had gotten through it before we had. "Yeah," I called back cautiously.

No response, but curiosity had already grabbed me by the ear and was pulling me toward the side of the house. Over the grass, a jump over the hole from my digging yesterday, and feet crunching hard over pavement and gravel—

And there she was. A girl, probably around my age, sitting in the soup pot. I blinked. She was too big to fit in the soup pot, so she was awkwardly tilted back into it, her butt in the pothole and her legs and arms balancing her from falling over.

I noticed the outfit first because it was identical to an outfit Isabella Lynch had worn last week. Loose, baggy pants that cinched at her waist and flared at her legs in a shade of mustard yellow. I'd thought that nothing could possibly go with pants like that, but Isabella—and this girl—had paired it with a tight shirt striped vertically in olive green and mahogany brown that somehow went perfectly. To carry it all, she wore simple plain white sneakers. Isabella's had been fashionably scuffed, while this girl's were bright white and pristinely clean.

What an odd coincidence. Maybe they'd both bought the outfit off the same mannequin?

"Could you help me to my feet?" the girl asked, her voice ringing in my head like a bell. It sounded familiar, though I couldn't place how. "I can't seem to stand."

She could've said please, but I moved forward anyway, my eyes searching her face. Brown hair curled wildly around it in a perfectly-mussed-beach-waves sort of way. Her eyes shone clear and hazel gold over rosy cheeks and plump pink lips and a . . . a perfect Disney-princess nose . . .

No. No way. It couldn't be.

I stopped in my tracks a few feet from the girl. "How did you get here?" I asked her, my stomach churning.

She laughed, and that's when I saw it. Her tongue, a pale petal pink . . . stamped in black with the letters of the *shem*.

"You put me here," she said, as though it were obvious. *No. Way.* "It would be very rude of you to leave me like this."

I stared down at her, my mind sparking all over the place, but somehow, my arm extended itself. She grabbed my hand. I wasn't sure what I expected hers to feel like—dirt? Cement?—but it was warm and squishy and bony, just like a real human hand.

She pulled hard, and I staggered, nearly dragged to the ground beside her. But she rose, her back lifting itself off the ground. I got the feeling that she didn't actually need my hand to stand up, she just wanted it. Maybe she wanted to see if our hands felt alike.

And then she was standing there in front of me, her feet spaced on either side of the soup pot, dusting those human hands on her pants. "So," she said. "What next?"

I blinked hard, like if I blinked hard enough, she would simply poof out of existence. She didn't. I tried again. Still there. So I probably wasn't losing my mind.

Which left no other explanation. Zaide's story had been true. And I had done it. Created a golem. It was hard to describe the mixture of pride and relief and excitement and terror that whooshed through me, blowing me up like a balloon. I had created a life that I was responsible for, on a much bigger scale than the egg babies we carried around last year for home ec, but maybe I'd *actually* solved my problem. The golem would live with Zaide and take care of him, and nothing would have to change.

"Hi," I said. "I'm Leah. Um, Leah—"

"Leah Roslyn Nevins. I know who you are." She smiled wide; her eyes glimmered with hope. "I'm not supposed to name myself, but I have. Is that okay?"

What was she doing, asking me for permission? I was just a kid. I didn't have to give anyone permission to do anything. I didn't have the authority to do that, unless you were, like, five years old. I could definitely boss around a five-year-old. "Sure," I said faintly.

"Good!" she said cheerfully. Her eyes sparkled with happiness. "Then my name is Elsa Aurora Ariel Belle."

Those were Disney-princess names. To go with her Disney-princess nose. If she introduced herself by her full name, people would wonder what the heck was going on. "Maybe you should just go by Elsa," I said.

Elsa, which wasn't really a Jewish name. Then again, was the golem Jewish? I hadn't thought about that as I made her. Did that mean she wasn't? Then again *again*, lots of Jews didn't have traditionally Jewish names. I did, but it wasn't like Lexy or Julie or Matilda were especially biblical.

Elsa's brow furrowed over her nose for a moment, like she was going to get angry at my comment on her name. I braced myself for an explosion, but the clouds cleared up, and she went back to smiling. "Whatever you say."

"Okay," I said uncertainly. "Okay. Well. We should probably come up with a cover story, right?"

She tilted her head, still smiling away. It was starting to get a little creepy, honestly. "A cover story?"

I gestured in front of me like my hands might be able to spell it out in the air. "You know. A story that says who you are, how I know you, what you're doing here, all that. So my family doesn't get suspicious."

She shook her head, her smile fading a little. "That's easy. I am a golem, created last night by you in the light of the moon and the damp of the dew, and my name is Elsa Aurora Ariel Belle. I am here because you wanted me here."

"Yes, but . . ." I let out a frustrated sigh. "That's the real story, but not the cover story. There's no way my parents will believe the real story. They'll think I'm a little kid making things up. We need to tell them something that sounds true and that they won't find suspicious."

The golem—Elsa—looked confused again.

"Leah? Leah?" Voices drifted over from the front yard. Matty's and Jed's. I hadn't even heard them pull up, but Mom and Dad must have told them I was waiting for them outside. It was only a matter of seconds before they found me. I needed to figure out a cover story right away.

So naturally, my mind wiped itself blank. *Think!* I screamed mentally at myself. *Think, um . . . What's your name again?*

I was doomed.

Matty and Jed rounded the corner, their faces breaking into smiles as they caught sight of me. "Hey, Leah!" Matty said. *Leah. Right.* Matty waved at the golem. "Hi!

I don't think we've met. I'm Matilda, and this is Jed. Are you a friend of Leah's?"

The golem shook her head. "Nope! I'm a—"

"She's joking!" I interrupted, forcing a laugh that came out sounding more like a bark. "Ha! Ha-ha! Isn't she funny?" I slung an arm over the golem's shoulders and squeezed, which distracted her enough to keep her from naysaying me. "Yes, she's my friend. She . . . lives on this block, too. Her name is Elsa."

"Hi, Elsa!" Jed said, but Matty looked a little skeptical.

"We've been visiting here every Saturday our whole lives, and we've never met any other kids living on this block."

"Right," I said, my mind racing for an excuse because of course that was all true. "Well. See. Elsa's always lived here, but her family always had something to do on Saturdays." My mind blanked again. I knew it was a bad idea before the words even left my mouth, but you've got to understand—I had no other options aside from standing there and letting my mouth open and close silently and stupidly like a guppy until I literally sank into the earth and died. "Elsa, what was it again?"

She had the whitest teeth I'd ever seen. "Skydiving," she said without hesitation.

That one word was enough to jar my mind back into making sense again. "Skydiving? Is that the best you could—" I suddenly realized how Jed and Matty were looking at us. Eyebrows pinched, eyes wary, nostrils a little bit flared: caution. "I mean, right! Skydiving, that's it. Yes." I turned back to Jed and Matty, nodding vigorously. "Elsa's family are all skydiving enthusiasts, and they used to go every single Saturday until . . . um, Elsa's mom's parachute broke."

"Oh my God!" Jed and Matty said together. Matty cupped her mouth with her hands. "Elsa, I'm so sorry."

Elsa cocked her head. "For what?"

"Right, her mom didn't die!" I said, letting out a maniacal cackle. I was beginning to feel a little bit like a maniac, actually. "So Elsa's not sad. She just . . . um, broke both legs. So she's okay, but the family can't go skydiving for a while. Out of respect for her mom, who can't get out of bed. So now Elsa is free to come hang out with us on Saturdays!"

I was breathing hard by the time my speech was over, like I'd just finished running a race. I kind of felt like I'd been running, actually, though I wasn't sure what I was trying to catch up with.

"Skydiving is very scary," Elsa said solemnly. "To be disconnected from the earth like that is a frightening thing."

Matty blinked. ". . . Okay," she said. "I thought maybe she'd just moved here or something, but that's certainly more interesting."

Ugh. I had to fight to keep myself from slapping one palm to my forehead. I couldn't believe I hadn't thought of that, but now I just had to roll with it. "Elsa does lead an interesting life," I said, and shot her a *look* not unlike the one the Three Ds kept giving one another. This look said, *Don't you dare say you've barely led a life at all, or I'll pull the* shem *out of your mouth and watch you crumble into dust.*

"I do," Elsa agreed. She winked and nudged me with her elbow, all like, *Look how good I did the lie,* but that was better than the alternative.

"Elsa, are you going to come in and have lunch?" Jed asked.

I started, "Oh, Elsa actually has to go home and spoon-feed her poor mother—" but the golem interrupted me with a squeal.

"Yes! I would love to eat some human food with you," Elsa said, trotting toward the front of the house.

I watched her go. *She just needs some time to adjust*, I told myself. *Less than twenty-four hours ago she was dirt, and now she's a person. I would need some time to figure things out, too.*

"Well, we've got chicken salad!" Jed called after her, then turned to me and said with a laugh, "Hopefully by 'human food' she doesn't mean actual humans."

It took me a moment to laugh in response.

CHAPTER EIGHT

I RAN AFTER ELSA AND managed to catch up with her before she made it inside Zaide's house. Matty and Jed were lagging behind, so it was safe for me to lean in and say through clenched teeth, "You need to follow my lead."

Elsa scanned the front of Zaide's old telephone building. "This is an odd house."

"Did you hear me?"

"What are you guys waiting for?" Matty and Jed had caught up. "Aren't you hungry?"

But inside, Dad and Aunt Jessie were sitting side by side on the couch waiting for us. Their features were fogged with worry; they looked in our direction, but as if they were trying to see something twenty feet behind us. "Is everything okay?" I asked.

The corners of my dad's lips turned up, but it was not a smile. "Everything's fine," he said. He took a deep breath, like he was preparing to say something else, but nothing came out except for a long, low exhale.

Aunt Jessie pursed her lips. Matty and Jed got their turquoise eyes from her—hers now shone sadly from her round face. "Aunt Caroline and Dad are sitting in the kitchen with Zaide for a bit," she said, the words aimed at Jed and Matty but her face aimed at me. My stomach clenched. I knew what that meant: that Zaide was confused again. That he was asking where Ruthie was or that he thought Mom was his dead daughter, and they didn't want us to face him when he didn't know who we were.

Dad's eyes focused on the golem. "Hello," he said, rising into an uncomfortable-looking half stand. "I'm Leah's dad."

"I know," the golem chirped. "I'm Elsa Aurora Ariel Belle, and I'm here because my mother—"

"Is very ill, bedridden," I interrupted. Jed and Matty might have bought the whole skydiving story, but I didn't think my dad would.

Elsa's smile didn't waver. "Exactly what she said."

"Oh, honey." Aunt Jessie rose and enveloped her in a hug. "I'm so sorry."

"You're welcome at our house as much as you want," Dad said over Aunt Jessie's shoulder. "We're just down the block, the green house with the white trim."

Yes. I gave my fist a victorious little pump. Now I had an excuse for the golem being around all the time. Parents couldn't help but sympathize with a motherless kid. I bet Mom would cry.

Now I just had to get her in with Zaide.

"Maria?" The voice was lost, confused, Yiddish, lispy.

We all turned toward the kitchen. Zaide stood there in the doorway, his jaw dropped as far as it could go. He was always pale, but somehow he'd gone even paler, like all the blood had drained to his neck, which was currently as red as a stop sign.

He looked like he'd seen a ghost.

"Maria?" he repeated, taking a step forward. My mom and Uncle Marvin appeared over his shoulders, one over each. Mom was biting her lip. Her face pinched in confusion when she saw the golem, but she didn't say anything.

He couldn't be talking to me, right? No matter how

confused he got, he wouldn't mistake me for someone else. Somehow that felt even worse than being forgotten altogether.

Zaide raised a trembling arm and pointed it at the golem. "Maria, how are you here?" He said something rapidly in another language—Yiddish or Polish by the sound of it.

The golem said something back. Her *shem*-inscribed tongue danced easily over the unfamiliar syllables. I gaped at her. I hadn't created her to know any other languages—maybe that was a golem superpower? Or maybe, since she was created partially from the soil of the old country, she knew those languages, too?

I didn't know. The only thing I knew was the effect her words had on Zaide: He sagged backward, his face collapsing on itself almost as if it were melting. Thank goodness Mom and Uncle Marvin were standing behind him to catch him. Otherwise he might have fallen on the floor and broken a hip.

"Why don't we go outside?" Dad and Aunt Jessie stood at the same time, blocking our view of Zaide—and Zaide's view of the golem.

It quickly became clear that Dad wasn't actually asking. He put one arm around my shoulders and the other around Elsa's. Aunt Jessie did the same for Jed and Matty, even though Jed was taller than she was, and together they steered us outside. I took a deep breath of the cold air. It tasted as refreshing as a drink on a hot day.

"Who's Maria?" Matty's voice was small. She looked a little bit like she'd seen a ghost, too.

"I don't know," Dad said. "Somebody from Zaide's past, probably. Maybe he knew a Maria when he was young."

Aunt Jessie turned to the golem. "Is your family Polish?"

The golem looked at me. I inclined my chin the tiniest bit. She looked Polish enough, come to think of it—we had some neighbors who'd moved here from Poland in our old neighborhood, and they'd had similar heart-shaped faces and high cheekbones.

"Yes," the golem said. "Polish skydivers. That's my family."

What had she said to Zaide, though, that had made him look so upset? I made a note to ask her next time we were alone together.

"Which house is yours?" my dad asked, thankfully not seizing upon the skydivers comment. "I didn't realize any Poles lived in the neighborhood."

The golem looked to me again for an answer. I didn't

have one. The chances were too great that, if I named a random house, my dad would know the people who actually lived there. He liked to chat with the joggers and the dog walkers while he was out doing yard work.

"The white house," Elsa said. Half the houses on the street were white.

"Which white—"

"Why don't we kick around a soccer ball?" I interrupted, my heart racing. Having a golem was a lot of work. Certainly a lot more work than my egg baby had been. "There's still that one in the bushes, right?"

"I love human sports!" said the golem.

Everybody stood and blinked at her for a moment, as if not quite sure how to respond to a statement like that.

"Me too!" I supplied. "I love human sports! Much better than squirrel sports or worm sports!"

Everybody laughed. Relieved, I jogged over to the holly bush and managed to extract the old soccer ball from beneath it without pricking myself on any of the leaves. The six of us separated into two teams that we tried to make fair—Matty, Dad, and Aunt Jessie on one, and me, Jed, and Elsa on the other. Jed and Matty were easily the best players: Matty was maybe a tiny bit more skilled, but Jed had longer legs. Dad was better than

Aunt Jessie, but they were both pretty terrible. Elsa was a wild card, and I was the worst.

Seriously, the worst. Even when I had a clear shot standing in front of the goal, my foot aimed at the ball, I missed half the time. And running around the field without tripping? The only reason I got an A in gym at Schechter was because the teacher pitied me for falling over my own feet and creating a pileup on the field so big the other kids spent the rest of the marking period asking me if I'd "had a good trip" and saying that they'd "see me next fall."

Maybe Elsa would be worse than me. That would be exciting.

Ten minutes later, I had to admit the truth: Elsa was not worse than me. Not only was she not worse than me, she wasn't worse than Aunt Jessie or Dad. She wasn't worse than Jed. She wasn't worse even than Matty.

She was better than all of them. She danced over the field like she was floating rather than kicking her way through grass and dirt; she twisted and twirled around us when we tried to steal the ball, and her kicks always went exactly where she aimed them. I paused at one point to watch her go head-to-head over the ball with Matty. They danced back and forth like they were participating in a waltz or something, Elsa bobbing and Matty weaving, then Elsa weaving while Matty bobbed. Matty stuck her leg out to try to steal the ball from Elsa; Elsa rolled it back just enough that Matty fell short, and then she feinted left. Matty dove toward the left, and Elsa lunged right with the ball, sending it sailing between Dad's legs and into our makeshift goal.

I was dumbstruck. "I can't believe you beat Matty!" I said, rushing to the golem's side as Dad jogged off to get the ball. Elsa wasn't even sweating. "Nobody's ever beaten Matty except for Jed!"

"Matilda," Matty reminded me. I avoided her eyes, and finally she looked away, over at Elsa. "But she's right. What team do you play on? You have to be on at least your school team. You're so good!"

"I am good at many things," the golem said, sniffing a little bit, like, *How dare you suggest that I am only good at one thing, you peasant.*

Envy kindled inside me like a flame. I wished I could be that confident about anything. Just one thing, really. I just wanted one thing where I could say *I'm so good at this* and mean it, and everybody would nod along with me because they could see it, too.

As soon as you're eighteen and you get that nose job, I

told myself. Then I could be confident. It was hard to be confident right now when I knew the first thing people saw when they looked at me was this honker.

We played a few more games. Elsa's team won every time. I quickly realized I shouldn't even bother trying. I jogged back and forth on the field, aiming my face toward the soccer ball. If it hit me in the face and broke my nose, maybe my parents would let me get that nose job while I was getting it fixed.

The ball did not hit me in the face even once, which was a disappointment.

By the time we finally wrapped up, Mom and Uncle Marvin had come outside and were cheering us on. "You can't cheer for both teams!" Jed shouted as he kicked the ball toward the goal. It flew past Aunt Jessie's feet and went in. Mom and Uncle Marvin erupted in boos.

Parents thought they were just so funny.

When the last game was done, Matty, Jed, and my aunt and uncle kissed us all goodbye and piled into their car. We watched them drive off. "Elsa, where do you live again?" Mom asked. "We can take you home, or else you're welcome to come over for dinner."

"I'll walk her home," I said quickly. Mom gave me a look, the one that said, *Leah, you're being rude.* I was going to get a talking-to later, but I could handle that. What I could not handle was another few hours trying to run interference around the golem.

The golem smiled at my parents. "Thank you for having me. I had a great time."

Great. Now Mom won't just talk about how rude I was, she'll talk about how rude I was compared to how polite the golem was. I grabbed Elsa's arm and pulled her in the opposite direction of our house, walking with her down the sidewalk until my parents disappeared through our front door. With the fear of them seeing us gone, I tugged Elsa beneath a tree in somebody's yard.

"Okay, you're not doing so bad," I said. "But what did you say to Zaide before that made him look so sad?"

"I know I'm not doing bad. I'm doing good," she said. "And all I told him was that he was mistaken and that I wasn't Maria, I was Elsa."

Okay. Good. As long as she hadn't said anything mean. I hadn't thought she had, but you couldn't be too sure. "Good," I said. "It's probably good you can speak to him in the old languages, anyway, since the whole reason I created you was to take care of Zaide."

She tilted her head. Her hair fell like a shimmering waterfall. "Take care of him?" she repeated.

"Take care of him, like, make sure he's doing well and is safe," I said. "Can you do that?"

She gave me the stink-eye. "I can do many things."

"Is that a yes or a no?"

She shrugged elegantly. "You created me. You give me my orders. So I must say yes."

"Okay, good," I said, relaxing a little bit and filing a mental note that she had to obey me. She'd said she was good at a lot of things. I'd seen her at soccer, and she wasn't exaggerating. She would do a great job taking care of Zaide, and he wouldn't have to go into the nursing home, and Matty and Jed and I would keep hanging out every Saturday afternoon until forever, and I would keep training at chess until I could beat Zaide every time. "So here's what I was thinking . . ."

As we walked back, I laid out the rules as I saw them. First and foremost: Take care of Zaide. Keep him from hurting himself or freaking out or, equally as important, calling my parents or aunt and uncle, because they had to know he was doing fine. Sit with him when he was confused and don't let him wander or climb up on the roof. Second: Don't freak Zaide out. Try to stay hidden as much as possible. Third: Report back to me, like this was a job and I was her boss.

She nodded after each one. "Got it, boss," she said, and saluted. It seemed a little bit like she was making fun of me, but her face was serious.

I nodded back. "Okay. Thank you. The door to Zaide's should be unlocked, soldier."

I watched her go. Trepidation simmered in my stomach, but I pushed the worry away. What could go wrong?

CHAPTER NINE

IT WAS MONDAY MORNING, AND I was at lunch because some heartless school administrator decided that sixth graders needed to have lunch at ten thirty in the freaking morning. That school administrator deserved to eat nothing but mushy peas and meatloaf-shaped cardboard—at ten thirty in the morning—for the rest of their days.

Anyway. I was sitting at the table with Deanna, Dallas, and Daisy, mechanically chewing my turkey sandwich. I wasn't really hungry yet, but otherwise, I'd be starving by the time school let out at 2:27. Deanna was telling us all how she'd spent the weekend helping her older brother move into his new town house. "And then the neighbor's pit bull broke free and charged at my sister, and she screamed and dropped the microwave on her foot, but it turned out the pit bull just wanted to lick her and get pet."

"Pit bulls are actually nice dogs," Dallas said, squinting down at her pudding cup to make sure she'd scraped out every single bit of the chocolaty goodness. "They have a bad rap because some jerks train them bad."

"Yeah." Deanna nodded. "The dog was nice. My sister had to go to the hospital for her foot, though."

We all winced in sympathy. Looking down, I noticed something on the table. Someone had carved a heart with *AP + JB* on the inside. I racked my brain for kids I knew with those initials but came up empty. I traced the letters with my finger and wondered how long they'd been here.

"Leah?"

I looked up. The Three Ds were all staring at me, inquisitive sets of brown and hazel and blue. All those eyes on me made my cheeks go hot. "What?" I blurted.

"I was just asking how your weekend was," Dallas said. Her voice sounded cautious, the way my mom's had when she talked about Zaide moving in with us. Like she was afraid of me or afraid of talking to me.

She didn't like me. I knew it.

I had gone a weirdly long time without answering. I had to be careful not to say anything that would make them like me even less, where I'd have to move to another lunch table. I couldn't sit at a lunch table by myself. That would be even worse than sitting at a table with people who weren't crazy about me. I could just imagine the whispers. *Look at that girl with the beak, all on her own. What a loser. I wouldn't let such a freak sit with us. Maybe not even if she got a nose job.*

And now I'd gone even weirdly longer without answering. "Oh, it was good," I said. Usually I stopped there, but I actually had something interesting to say today. "I . . . met a new neighbor who moved in down the street who's my age. It turns out she speaks Polish. And she's really good at soccer—she kicked my and my cousins' butts."

"Nice," Daisy said. She actually sounded like she meant it. "Is she going to be coming to our school?"

I hadn't thought about that. The back of my neck heated up, then my cheeks. "Um, I don't know," I said. "She might be going to private school."

"That's a shame." Deanna sighed. "Our soccer team could use some players who are actually good."

Dallas elbowed her in the side, using all the arm strength she didn't get to use playing for our school soccer team. Deanna shrieked a laugh, and just like that, they were batting at each other, Dallas finally stealing a victory by swiping Deanna's pretzel sticks. "I'll give them back if you say pretty please," Dallas said, dangling them just out of reach.

Back on the outside again, I checked my phone for any messages from Lexy and Julie. We'd talked a little bit over the weekend about planning a get-together, but future weekends were busy. They had a lot of stuff going on: Purim preparations and things to do with stupid Naomi. It was pretty sad, thinking about it, how I was orbiting on the outside of two different friend groups right now.

I wasn't going to let Lexy and Julie drift away, though. I texted them *my insides feel like gummy worms right now you guys*—an inside joke—and tucked my phone back away. They couldn't share that one with Naomi. *She* hadn't been there.

"Leah?"

I jerked my head up. The Three Ds were looking at me *again*. "Yeah?" I said, trying to sound nonchalant.

"You said you were playing soccer with your neighbor," Dallas said. "Do you play, like, for real?"

I snorted. "No, I'm terrible." Then I blushed because maybe I didn't want to share how terrible I was at anything when I wanted people to like me. "I mean, maybe not terrible, but not good enough to play on a school team."

"Oh," Dallas said, sounding disappointed. "Well, do you play any other sports?"

I shook my head. "Not really." There weren't too many sports where "falling over your feet" was a positive. "Unless you count chess as a sport, I guess. I like chess."

Deanna shrieked and pounded her fist on the table. "No way! You play *chess*?"

I could feel the earlier blush draining out of my face, leaving me sickly pale. Oh no. Had I just admitted to something that would get me made fun of?

"I *love* chess!" Deanna exclaimed, her whole face lighting up. I relaxed, becoming hopefully slightly less sickly pale. She elbowed Dallas beside her. "I've been trying to convince these nerds to start up a chess club with me so that I could play with someone other than the old people at the library, but they won't bite."

Daisy rolled her eyes. "*We're* the nerds?"

Deanna smiled big at me, so big she showed the edges

of her gums. "This is so exciting. Leah, we have to play sometime."

I gave her a tiny smile in response. I wasn't sure if I could play chess with anyone other than Zaide. It would feel like betraying him. And what if I was actually terrible at chess, too, and Zaide just hadn't wanted to make me feel bad? Then Deanna would think I was an idiot, which meant the other two Ds would think I was an idiot, too.

My phone buzzed. I grabbed for it, relieved to have an excuse to look away. Julie had messaged me back. *So weird mine are feeling like celery stalks??* Another inside joke. My smile stretched, growing as wide as Deanna's. Or at least I thought they were the same. I was too busy looking at my phone.

Nothing notable happened the rest of the day, except that Isabella Lynch spilled something down her front during lunch and walked around all day with a bright red splotch on her white shirt and didn't even seem self-conscious about it. I didn't have to stay after for anything, so I went home and stretched out on the couch in front of the TV, turning on some anime. As soon as

I heard the rumble of the garage door, I jumped off the couch, turned the TV off, and spread my textbooks and binders out on the table in front of me. I picked up my pencil just as my mom walked through the door.

I set it down, sighing and flexing my fingers as I did, like they were cramped after working for hours. "Hi, Mom."

"Hi, hon." She sat down at the table with a heavy sigh. "How was school?"

I literally always answered that question the same exact way. "School was fine."

"Good. Are you almost done with your homework?"

I shut my binder with a snap. "Basically." I could always do it during homeroom tomorrow.

"Good."

"Did you go to Zaide's today?" I asked. Mom usually stopped by his house every single day. To check on him, she said, and make sure he was doing okay. I half suspected it was because Zaide was very old, and she just wanted to make sure he wasn't dead on the floor.

"Not yet," she said. "I was just stopping home to drop off my stuff before heading over. Want to come?"

"Sure," I said casually, even as my heart leaped. I hadn't

heard from the golem since I left her there on Saturday. This would be the first time I'd get to see what sort of job she was doing.

At first look, she seemed to be doing well. Mom and I walked through Zaide's front door and shouted "Hello!" and were greeted by Zaide, who sounded in good spirits and didn't ask who we were. We walked in farther to find him sitting on the red velvet couch, the TV showing something in black and white. I didn't even realize they still showed TV in black and white.

Before stepping forward to give Zaide his customary kiss on the cheek, I performed a surreptitious sweep of the room with my eyes. No golem in sight.

Maybe she'd nodded and smiled and hadn't come here after all. She could have lied about needing to obey me. Worry pricked me. I hadn't actually watched her go inside Zaide's house. I'd told her to wait outside and go in at night, when it was dark and he'd be sleeping. She could be anywhere right now.

"I was just about to make some tea," Zaide said when I pulled away.

"I'll make some," my mom said, already moving off toward the kitchen. I trailed after her, looking around for any sign of the golem. I wasn't sure exactly what I was looking for, but I didn't see anything that made me think she was here.

Except . . . "Wow, look how neat Zaide's desk is," Mom said, raising her eyebrows as we passed by. Indeed, the desk usually covered by stacks of paper and scattered scraps was now neatly organized, piled with file folders that even had colored tabs in them. They looked a little bit like the binders I used for school. "It's about time— I've been telling him to organize it for ages. I was starting to think I'd have to do it after . . . Well, let's not think about that." *After he died*, she meant. I gave the desk a beady eye. Golem work?

Mom's surprise didn't fade away in the kitchen. "Wow!" she said, running a finger over the table. "I think this is the first time in my life it's not all sticky!" Not only was the table's surface not sticky, it was free of coffee rings and crumbs and dirty plates. There weren't even any plates in the sink. Golem work?

Mom put the water on to boil and went in search of Zaide's tea bags. "I'm going to go to the bathroom," I announced.

"Have a party," she said in response.

I was not going to have a party, but I also was not going to the bathroom. Not like I would've had a party in the bathroom anyway. I had no idea why my mom said things like that. I waited until my mom's head was fully submerged in the cabinet and then darted in the opposite direction. With Zaide staring at the TV and the volume blasting for his poor half-deaf ears, it was easy to open and close the door of the second bedroom without anyone noticing.

The second bedroom was probably the place in Zaide's house I'd been in least, simply because there was never much of a reason to go in there. Most of my bubbe Ruth's old things were stored in here: her antique sewing machine and sewing basket filled with scraps of fabric and pincushions porcupined with needles, a closet full of old-lady dresses and hats. The bed sat in the middle of the small room, taking up a good half of the space.

From under the bed stretched a lock of brown hair like a sea creature extending a leg from the water. I crouched down cautiously and looked beneath the bed. The golem stared back. "Um, hello," I said. I didn't think I had to worry about anyone overhearing me, what with the TV on extra loud, but I lowered my voice anyway. "How are you doing?"

"Fine," the golem said back. She spoke so quietly I had to lean in to hear her, contorting my neck uncomfortably, but I figured it was the least I could do. "He's a nice old guy. I cleaned everything up for him. The house was pretty messy."

"Thanks," I said. "Everything looks really good."

"Yeah, it does." Again, I was struck by her confidence. How she didn't even have to thank me for the compliment, because I was just telling her something she already knew. "He got a little bit confused last night, but I stuck with him and stopped him from doing anything that might hurt him." She pushed out her lower lip, but not like she was sad—like she was deep in thought. "I'm pretty sure he thinks I'm a ghost."

"That's okay," I said. It didn't matter what he thought she was, if she could calm him, keep him safe, and stop him from doing anything that might panic Mom and Dad. "Thank you."

She blinked at me like an owl. "You don't have to thank me. This is what you created me to do."

"I know," I said, but the thought of not thanking her for doing this massive thing for me made me squirm inside. "I still mean it, though."

She shrugged as best she could while hiding under the bed. In practice, it meant she shimmied around a little bit like there was something with a lot of legs trying to crawl up her shirt. "Whatever," she said, and her tone made it clear that the conversation was over.

She wasn't the boss, though. "Keep it up," I said. "Keep doing the same things, and we'll all be fine."

She worked herself farther beneath. The tendril of brown hair sucked itself under the bed and vanished.

Outside the room, the volume of the TV had lowered, and Mom and Zaide were talking. Well, Zaide was talking, and Mom was yelling. I paused, the door half-open.

"Did you think about what we discussed last time?" Mom shouted directly into his ear.

Zaide didn't turn to look at her, just kept staring at the TV. "Yes."

"And what did you think?" Mom smiled encouragingly. "Wasn't the facility I showed you nice? You'd be able to keep most of your independence, and—"

"I won't go."

My heart lifted. Zaide was on my side after all. And nobody could beat Zaide when he set his mind to something. *Checkmate, Mom.*

"Zaide, we're worried about you," Mom said. And she did sound worried, but that didn't mean she knew what was best for him. "How can we—"

"I renovated this place from the ground up. Everything but the outside walls and cement floor, I built," Zaide said. "I'm staying in my home, and that's the end of that."

I gave myself a silent fist pump of victory, which bumped into the door and made it creak all the way open. Mom turned to look at me, and her brow furrowed. "What are you doing in there?"

I shrugged, stepping out and closing the door behind me. "Nothing." No need for Zaide to find Elsa living under the bed and have a heart attack. I noticed the two steaming cups of tea on the coffee table. "Where's mine?" I asked.

"In the kitchen," Mom said. "I only have two hands."

I snorted. "Keep up the human disguise, you Jewish octopus."

I heard her laughing darkly as I went toward the kitchen. The people who hated Jews—there were, unfortunately, a lot of them—sometimes drew us as octopuses spreading our tentacles across the continents because, apparently, we controlled the world or wanted to control the world or whatever.

We had to turn it into a joke because if we didn't turn it into a joke, it meant too much thinking seriously about how many people hated people like me even though they didn't know me. They hadn't even seen my nose.

Stop thinking about that, I told myself. Focus on the good things. The golem was maybe literally a godsend. She was doing everything she was supposed to do, and maybe some jerks half the world away or in the next town wanted me dead, but that didn't matter right now. They could hate me all they wanted.

One thing at a time. As long as the golem was working out, that would be enough for now. As we said at the Passover seder: *dayenu*.

CHAPTER TEN

I GOT HOME LATE FROM school on Thursday because I had a chorus rehearsal, and Mom and Dad were already home talking in the kitchen. I crept up the hallway so that they wouldn't hear me, because sometimes—no, I'd say most of the time—eavesdropping is the best way to get information from your parents. It had worked before—it wasn't like they would have volunteered on their own that they wanted to lock Zaide up in a nursing home.

"... something's changed," Mom was saying. "His house is so clean. He hasn't seemed any worse than confused when I went over there. No distress calls in the middle of the night."

"That's great," Dad replied. "Maybe it's a change for good."

"We can only hope."

Nobody else could see me, and there was nothing to knock into this time, so I let myself do it: a victory fist pump, and not just a baby one, a big one from my face all the way to my chest. *So long, nursing home.*

The afterglow of victory lasted well into the next day. Friday was always a good one at school because everybody knew we wouldn't have to be there the next day. The Three Ds were all smiles; one of Dallas's moms was extremely pregnant, and Dallas was hoping she'd get a new sibling soon.

"It's going to be a boy," Dallas was saying, practically bouncing up and down in her seat. Her cheeks were a bright, excited red against her pale skin and hair. "I told them they should name him Noah because Noah is an adorable name. Or Joey. I just like two syllable names."

Daisy squealed, her long black hair swinging as she clasped her hands under her chin. "Babies are so cute."

"Have you ever actually met a baby?" Deanna asked, wrinkling her nose. "Babies are gross and annoying. All they do is eat and cry and poop." Deanna had two much-younger siblings in addition to her older brother and sister, so she would know.

"Yeah, but they're soooo cute while they're doing it," Daisy said with a sigh. Daisy was an only child like me.

Deanna grumbled something like, *You're welcome to have my siblings*, and they all started arguing. I smiled along with them, nodding when I thought I should, until some movement caught my eye over Daisy's shoulder.

A few of the seventh-grade boys were hurling french fries at one another at the opposite end of the room, and the lunch aides were throwing themselves selflessly into the lines of battle. Probably to save Isabella Lynch, who was presiding over a table nearby.

I glanced quickly over at that table to make sure she hadn't been hit, then away. Looking at her and her friends was dangerous, like looking directly at the sun. Except the danger here wasn't going blind, it was them catching me looking at them. Not that they'd say anything or do anything major, but whoever saw me would get that little wrinkle between their eyebrows that meant *scorn*, and they'd turn and whisper to the person next to them, and they'd turn around and look at you, too, with the raised eyebrows that meant *pathetic*, and so on. Just the thought of all of them staring at me with raised and wrinkled eyebrows was enough to make my nose sweat.

Today Isabella Lynch was wearing an oversize olive-green dress with shimmery, silver leggings underneath, all tied together with a black belt. I didn't own any dresses like that, but maybe I could borrow a dress from my mom and belt it tight at the waist. I'd seen outfits like that in videos I watched of the runways at the last New York Fashion Week.

Isabella Lynch tossed her dark hair over her shoulder and turned to whisper to the girl next to her. I didn't remember seeing this girl at the lunch table before. Did she even go here? She had brown hair, and—I squinted, and then my heart stuttered to a stop.

No.

No way.

"Leah," Dallas was saying. "You don't have any siblings, right?"

I couldn't believe what I was seeing. Dallas had to prompt me again before I stumbled out with an answer. "Only child here."

Are my eyes playing tricks on me?

Daisy gave me a high five. I caught it just a moment

too late, as her smile was beginning to flicker. "Here's to never having to share a room."

"So you'd be coming at this from an unbiased perspective," Dallas said. "What name do *you* like? Noah or Bartholomew?"

I didn't know anything about names. And this was *not* the time to be thinking about it. Not when a potential crisis was brewing across the room.

"Leah?" Dallas said.

It was the golem, just sitting there like she belonged. She saw me staring; my jaw might actually have fallen open. She smiled at me and gave me a little wave. That attracted Isabella's attention. Isabella waved at me, too, but she looked mystified, like she had no idea why she was doing it.

If the golem was here, what was Zaide doing? Before I could think too hard about the consequences, I gathered up my books and stood. "Are you okay?" Dallas asked.

"I just . . . Um, remember when I told you about my new neighbor? That's her over there." I was walking off before I heard Daisy asking, "But I thought you said she was going to private school?"

Isabella Lynch's whole table turned to look at me as I approached. The combined force of all those eyes—many mascaraed and eyelinered, unlike mine—was almost enough to make me falter. But then the golem grinned, and I filled up with anger, and that was enough to keep me forging on.

I kept my eyes fixed on hers. "Can I speak with you in private?" I said through clenched teeth. Everybody was still staring at me. Their conversation had hushed. I knew what they were all thinking. *What is she doing here? Look at that nose—isn't it huge? Does she really think she belongs here, at this table, with all of us? Shouldn't she know she just doesn't fit in?*

"These are my friends," the golem said, her voice ringing loud and clear. Even the Three Ds could probably hear her across the room. "Anything you want to say to me, you can say to them."

A muscle twitched in my jaw like it was going to try to burst free, showering Isabella Lynch and the golem and all the other kids with my blood and guts. "They are not your friends. You've known them for what, two minutes? Can I talk to you for a minute? *Now*?"

"You're being so mean," the golem said. Her eyes went wide, her lips trembly.

"Yeah, why are you being so mean to Elsa?" a girl across the table chimed in.

"Elsa *is* our friend," Isabella said. Up close, I could see her eyes were as dark as mine.

I took a deep breath. It stuck somewhere in my throat and didn't go all the way down to my lungs, which meant I started to get dizzy. I had to say something, but anything I could think of would come out sounding stupid. If I kept arguing with them about how Elsa wasn't really their friend, they would just double down on how mean I was, and I would become a complete social outcast. It wasn't like I could tell them that Elsa was a golem and I'd created her and she didn't belong here.

"I didn't mean to be mean," I said, and my voice came out froggy, like I was trying not to cry, even though I wasn't, but now that was the worst thing because everyone would think I was trying not to cry, and only babies cried at school. "I just . . . I didn't expect to see you here, and . . ."

I trailed off because I had no idea where else to go with that. I was standing there in front of Isabella Lynch and her friends, and they were all looking at me like I was an alien who'd just crashed through the cafeteria ceiling in a mini UFO, and—*oh God*—the Three Ds were probably staring at me from our usual table and whispering all like, *What's gotten into Leah? Is she losing her mind?*

I focused on the golem. A triumphant little smile was playing over her lips. She was doing this on purpose, I realized. I hadn't thought she was sophisticated enough to manipulate me like this. She hadn't been earlier—I couldn't picture the creature who spun that story about skydiving and talked about human food behaving like this. Was she evolving? Or playing dumb . . . which was also a form of manipulation?

When I'd created her, I *had* been thinking about how I wanted to be better at working other people . . .

Just as I was thinking that, she spoke. "It's okay. I understand. You guys," she said to the rest of the table. They all leaned in a little bit to hear her, the way flowers turn their faces to the sun. "Leah is my neighbor, and she's great. I should have asked her to sit with us. Leah, do you want to sit with us?"

The table was silent, and I died a little bit, but then everybody murmured in agreement, nodding along with the golem. "That wasn't what I was . . . ," I started, but the golem was already standing, and the girl on her other side was scooting down, and the golem was ushering me into my new seat next to her. One person away from Isabella Lynch.

Well. This wasn't what I was expecting, but . . . would it really be the worst thing to sit here for a little bit? It wasn't like the golem was going to rush out to Zaide's house right now anyway. Lunch was over in like ten minutes. Zaide could wait another ten minutes. But ten minutes could change *my* life. It wouldn't take nearly so long for Isabella Lynch to muse, *Leah, you have such a pretty face except for that nose. Please let me show you some ways to apply makeup to make it look smaller. We can be best friends then, and you'll belong.*

I sat. "Thanks," I said grudgingly to the golem because it would have seemed weird if I hadn't. I left my lunch in my bag. I'd finished most of it anyway, and who knew what Isabella Lynch and her friends would think of a turkey sandwich with pretzels and orange slices? Maybe they were vegetarians. Or allergic to citrus. I didn't want such a stupid thing as my lunch to make them think I was a loser, not when I already had this nose to battle.

"So, you're new, aren't you?" Isabella Lynch said to

me. She had her head cocked to one side, and she was looking at me that way you'd look at a new shirt you're thinking of buying in a store. "Both of you."

"We are," the golem said. She took a voracious bite of her pizza. I blinked. It was real pizza, a greasy triangle slice dotted with pepperoni, not the square white slice we could get from the cafeteria on Fridays. Where had she gotten that? I hoped she hadn't ordered it to Zaide's house. He kept kosher, and pepperoni was pork—something forbidden. It wasn't supposed to touch his dishes.

"Yeah," I said a moment too late. *Ugh.* Already starting out bad.

"Where are you from?" Isabella asked. She still seemed relaxed, didn't even raise an eyebrow at my faux pas. Whew.

"*I* was going to a school in Japan," the golem said breezily, taking another bite of her pizza. She chewed slowly and daintily, not getting so much as a drop of grease on her porcelain skin.

That distracted me for a minute from what she'd actually said. Japan. What?

"My family and I were traveling the world," she continued. The kids around the table were rapt, their attention on her like they were paper clips and she was a magnet. "My mother is a model and my father is a famous photographer, and they are always scouting new designers to model and new locations to photograph. So we were in Japan for a year. Before that, we were in Kenya. Before that, Sweden. Before that, Brazil. Before that . . ." She went on listing places, definitely more than twelve. She couldn't have logistically spent a year in all those places, but everybody nodded along like she made complete and total sense.

Isabella Lynch smiled when the golem finally stopped talking. "Of course your mom's a model, you're so pretty," she said. "Why'd you come *here*?"

The golem fluttered a hand through the air to the tabletop, a butterfly landing. "My great-grandparents were kings and queens of Lichtenstein, and the current rulers of Lichtenstein didn't like having us so close, because they worried we'd come to reclaim the throne. So we came to America, where everyone is supposed to be equal."

Lichtenstein? Was that even a real place? But beyond that, a backstory of royalty? That sounded familiar. I'd thought about wanting that when I was creating the—

"Lina?" Isabella was waving her hand in front of my

face. I snapped back. Oh no. She'd gotten my name wrong. It would be too embarrassing to correct her right now. I'd just have to change my name. Go by Lina for the rest of my life. It would be a shame. I liked my name. Leah was one of the biblical matriarchs in Judaism, so whenever the prayers talked about her, I got to pretend they were about me. I would miss that, but—

"It's actually Leah," the golem said, leaning forward and blocking my view of Isabella. "Her name."

"Oh, right. Sorry. That's pretty," said Isabella. The golem leaned back, and I found Isabella smiling at me. Really? That was it? That easy? Maybe just because the golem was the one who'd done it. Isabella thought she was a world-traveling model/princess, and I was definitely not. "Leah. Where are you from?"

I hoped I didn't say anything wrong this time. "Um . . ." was what came out, and not even in my regular voice—in a high pitch like I was about to start singing. *Good start, Leah. Way to not be embarrassing.* I cleared my throat. "I moved here at the beginning of the school year from Pickering. In New York. It's like two hours away."

"Pickering?" one of the other kids repeated. "Oh, I know Pickering. I used to live near there, too. That's the town with all the Jews with the long beards and black hats."

I tried not to sigh. By "all the Jews" she meant all the ultra-Orthodox Jews.

Schechter wasn't an ultra-Orthodox school, and I, obviously, was not ultra-Orthodox, or else I probably wouldn't be at a public school. Ultra-Orthodox Jews weren't the only Jews in Pickering, only the most noticeable. My family considered ourselves Conservative Jews, though that didn't mean conservative like in politics or dress—it was kind of like a denomination of our faith, like how a Christian could be Episcopalian or Baptist or Methodist. I thought of it as medium religious, between the hard-core Orthodox Jews and the more relaxed Reform Jews, but there were other, smaller pockets in there, too.

Isabella Lynch leaned forward, her brown eyes bright on mine. "What was that like? Living near all of them?"

"Well, I'm Jewish, too, but not *that* kind of Jewish." My words all tumbled out in a rush. I felt a twinge of guilt at the way I'd said it, like I was abandoning my people, but banished it. Hashem would understand.

Isabella's eyes brightened further. "Oh, you are? I didn't realize." She examined my face like she was a doctor and I was a patient; I shifted uncomfortably as her eyes bumped up the bridge of my nose, traveled over my thick eyebrows, crawled along the path of my hairline. "But you do look Jewish. So I shouldn't be surprised."

A girl on Isabella's other side dropped her sandwich in surprise, blinking in disbelief, like Isabella had said something incredibly insulting. I, too, was left with the vague feeling that she had, even though everything she'd said was true. I *was* Jewish. It shouldn't be an insult that I looked it, right?

"You have to come over to my house sometime," Isabella said, and just like that, the vague sense of unease vanished, replaced by a warm sparkly glow. Isabella Lynch. Invited. Me. Over to her house.

Be cool, Leah. Don't show too much enthusiasm. I wanted to nod like I was headbanging, but I limited it and said slowly, "Oh, sure. That would be fun."

"Maybe next week," Isabella continued. "On Monday? I have student government that day, and the late bus doesn't care if you take it home with me."

"Maybe," I said casually, like my insides weren't doing cartwheels and somersaults right now. "I'll check with my parents."

The bell dinged overhead. I crumpled my brown paper bag in on itself and floated after Isabella and her friends as they left the cafeteria. I glimpsed the Three Ds from the corner of my eye, and it looked like they were giving one another *looks* again, but I didn't care. I'd been invited over to Isabella Lynch's house! It took all the way till we were in the hallway outside, people breaking off to stop at their lockers, for me to remember that I really, really, really needed to talk to the golem.

I didn't bother trying to convince her this time. It hadn't worked at the table, and I was sure she'd discovered a way to outmaneuver me now, too. Instead, I waited until Isabella and most of the others were looking the other way, then grabbed the golem by her arm and yanked her behind a bank of lockers. She yelped, but the noise was lost in the clamor and din of the hallway.

Once I had her in a marginally more quiet location, I backed off and crossed my arms, fixing her with as intense a glare as I could manage. "What are you doing here?" Another thought occurred to me. "*How* did you even get here? You weren't on the bus. Where are you even going?" My stern tone faded into curiosity as I went on. "You're not enrolled in any of the sixth-grade classes. Nobody notices an extra face in the lunchroom, but any teacher is definitely going to notice a random new student showing up." Back to anger as I remembered why I was interrogating her in the first place. "And what about Zaide? You're supposed to be keeping him safe!"

She wilted a little bit. "How am I supposed to answer all of those questions? Should I just go in order?"

"I guess," I said.

She raised a hand and started ticking off her fingers. "One: What I'm doing here is meeting new people and having fun because I was bored. Two: How I got here is golem magic, and the specifics are none of your business. Three: Where I am going is through the hallway with my new best friends. I'm not going to class—that would be extremely boring. And four: Zaide is sleeping. He takes a nap every day around now for a couple hours because he wakes up at like four in the morning. Nothing bad is going to happen to him while he's sleeping.

"Besides," she continued. "I've kept him safe a *lot* already so far. Two nights ago he got all upset and tried to call the police because his wife was missing, and I stopped him. And the other day he wanted to go for a drive to some old soda shop that isn't there anymore, and I stopped that, too."

I couldn't help but soften a bit at her explanation.

Still. "What if he wakes up while you're here and wants to call the police again?"

Something flashed in her eyes. I couldn't tell what it was, but it unsettled my stomach a little. "He won't."

Okay, now my stomach was churning. "Is he . . . ? You didn't do anything to him, did you?"

Elsa rolled her eyes. "Oh my God, Leah, I did not kill your great-grandfather. He's just sleeping. Okay?"

"Okay," I said, taking a deep breath. "But you still shouldn't be here. I should . . ." I trailed off. What I was going to say was that I should give her new orders: to stay with Zaide no matter what. Because it was true, I'd given her orders to keep him safe, but I hadn't explicitly told her to stay by his side at all times. And it sounded like she was a little genielike, meaning she'd do *exactly* as I asked her but look for as many loopholes as she could.

But then I remembered lunch today. I wouldn't be able to sit with Isabella and her friends without Elsa. And I wanted to. I wanted to go over to Isabella's house on Monday and become her friend. I wanted to be popular and feel like I really belonged and fit in. I wanted people to think I was cool.

"I know what you're thinking," the golem said smugly. "You want me here."

I stiffened. Maybe I wanted her here, but I didn't have to act like it. "Whatever," I said. "As long as Zaide is okay, I don't care what you do."

Her smile widened, and for a moment, her rows of bright white teeth reminded me of a shark. "Wait," I said hastily. "I don't mean that. Your instructions are still to keep Zaide safe and okay, but if you would like to leave for a half hour while he's taking his nap and magically teleport here for lunch or whatever, I guess that would be fine."

She gave me a salute. This time I was sure she was mocking me. "Whatever you say, boss." She turned like she was going to go, except I blinked and she was no longer there. Okay, so she did have magic golem teleportation powers. That was kind of cool.

Not as cool as I was going to be, though. I hurried down the hallway after Isabella and her friends. I couldn't see them anymore, but if I walked fast enough, I could probably catch up.

CHAPTER ELEVEN

THE THREE DS STARED AT me when I took my seat back in class. I shrugged at them apologetically. It wasn't like they would care where I sat at lunch. They'd probably be happy to have their table back all to themselves.

Besides, my insides were all still fizzing and popping like a shook-up soda can. If I tried to talk, I would explode with excitement. I couldn't believe it was the golem that put all of this in motion.

Our teacher clapped her hands at the front of the room. Relieved, I turned to the front. The way the Three Ds were looking at me was making me squirmy. But there was nothing like a math test to jolt that feeling right out of you.

It came right back, though, when Deanna stopped at my desk just before the bell rang. "Hey," she said. She was smiling, but not as wide as usual. "So your friend goes to school here?"

"I guess so," I said. "She just kind of . . . appeared."

Deanna laughed, even though I hadn't been making a joke. Still, that made me feel bold enough to maybe make another joke. Also, it didn't matter as much what she thought of me now. I didn't have to stress out. I'd been invited over to *Isabella Lynch's house.* "I wish I could appear and disappear like that. Like, pop quiz?" I snapped my fingers. "Poof. Now I'm gone. Sorry, Ms. Bunce. You'll have to torture the rest of the class instead."

She laughed again. Kind of a warm feeling fluttered inside me. I realized I liked making her laugh. "Only if you take me with you."

The warm feeling turned into a kind of surprise. She'd really want to go with me? Or was she just saying that?

"I was thinking maybe you could come over one day soon." Deanna shifted her books from one arm to the other. "We could make plans for our chess club, and then Dallas and Daisy could come over afterward, because they're peasants who don't have the patience for the greatest game." She wrinkled her nose to show she was kidding.

"Chess club?" I asked.

"Yeah, remember? You said you might want to start one up."

I wanted to go over to Deanna's house, but was she just inviting me because she wanted someone else to play chess with? She'd just said her other friends didn't want to do it. And a chess club? That felt weird. It felt like taking my thing with Zaide and making it . . . not my thing with Zaide anymore. Like saying I'd given up on him. "Oh, I don't know," I said vaguely.

Something flickered over her face. After a moment, Deanna asked, "Is this because you're sitting with Isabella now?"

"What?" I asked, surprised. I felt a small pinch of guilt in my chest. "I—"

The late bell chirped. My next period teacher, Mr. Castro, was a stickler about timeliness. "I have to go," I said, hoisting my books up. "Can we talk about this later?" I was out of the room before I heard her response.

Mom and Dad weren't home when I got there, so I decided to stop by Zaide's. Mostly to say hi. Definitely not because I was worried that the golem had lied to me and she'd actually done something terrible to him while he was napping.

Yeah. Definitely not.

Zaide's door was unlocked, as always. I walked in quietly. Usually the only sound to greet me was the blaring TV, or the blasting radio, or sometimes the death-metal jangling of the phone as the Christmas lights lit up overhead in a blazing rainbow.

But not today. Today Zaide was speaking. On the phone? Had one of his other grandkids or great-grandkids called?

But no. Someone was speaking back, in rapid-fire Polish. Or Yiddish. The golem. I crept forward, still out of view.

I had no idea what they were saying. If they'd been speaking in Hebrew about a world or the night or any of the numbers between one and ten I could have picked that out, but I didn't know any Yiddish or Polish. The golem finished speaking, and Zaide dove right into his response. He spoke like I'd never heard him speak before, like he still had all his teeth and no waver from old age had set in. Like he was still young.

His words had a snap to them, too. And her answer was biting. Almost taunting. Like she was making fun of him.

I couldn't bear it. "Hello!" I announced as loud as I could, striding into the room with my arms held wide. I had no idea why I was doing that, but it felt good to take up as much space as possible. Like the more space I took up, the less there was for the golem.

Silence fell over them. I tried to catch one of their eyes, but they slid off me as if my own eyes were made of oil. "I'm here!" I announced again.

"Hello." Zaide said finally. He took a step toward me, and I blinked, and the golem wasn't there anymore.

My stomach churned with the feeling of *something's-notright*. I chose to believe it was the sudden absence of the golem, and not how Zaide didn't greet me with his usual "Leah Roslyn!"

He noticed her absence as well. "Maria? Where did you go?" Zaide said. Zaide looked around for the golem. His eyebrows pinched together, all the skin of his forehead with it. It looked uncomfortable.

Something'snotright something'snotright.

"Who's Maria?" I asked.

"Maria?" he echoed.

This is what I knew about Zaide's past: He didn't like to talk about how he'd escaped the Holocaust, but he and his parents and his two brothers had made it out of Poland and into America before the concentration camps opened, when America barred most of the fleeing Jews from its shores. They'd gotten lucky because his dad "knew someone," Zaide had vaguely said. I thought this maybe meant that his dad had bribed someone with a lot of money. He was twelve, like me, when he arrived, and his family bought a chicken farm not far from here. When he got older and found out the land under the chicken farm was worth a whole lot of money, he sold the chicken farm and became an electrician. At some point in there, he married Bubbe Ruth, and they had three children.

Oh, and before he left Poland, he created a golem.

I wondered what his golem had looked like. If it had a name. If he'd remembered to make it Jewish, or if he'd purposely made it not Jewish.

"Maria. You keep talking about her. You thought my friend Elsa was her," I said. His whole face was pinched up now. He was already upset. I might as well double down. "Was she someone from Poland?"

"Poland?" he echoed. His eyes were focused somewhere behind me, like he was looking at something far away.

"Yeah, Poland," I prompted. "From when you lived there?"

He squinted at me. "I'm sorry. I'm afraid I don't know what you're talking about." His voice was oddly formal. "Would you mind clarifying?"

A cold fist clutched my heart. "Zaide, it's me. Leah Roslyn. You know? You know me." He didn't look like he knew me. The fist squeezed hard. "Your great-granddaughter. You know?"

"Of course," Zaide said, but the fog didn't lift from his face. His warm brown eyes didn't focus on me, and his lips didn't split in a familiar smile as he said *Leah Roslyn!* "How can I help you?"

What was I supposed to do? Just run off and leave him here while he didn't know what was going on? He didn't seem angry, at least, just a little confused. He would probably be fine.

But what if he wasn't? What if he tried to turn on the TV and the signal was staticky and he decided he had to climb up on the roof to fix it?

The golem. She'd somehow managed him for the past week, and managed him well. I needed her help. Her guidance.

Wherever she was. "Elsa?" I said uncertainly, turning around in a circle. "Elsa, can you hear—"

I stopped and faced Zaide again, and Elsa was standing there like she'd never left. "What?" she said to me.

I gestured to Zaide, who was staring down at the golem with huge, liquid eyes. "He's confused. Help him."

"Maria?" he said. There was a tremble in his voice. "I thought you were—"

The golem burst out with something in rapid-fire Polish. Zaide fell silent. His shoulders drooped. He looked down at the floor.

"Is he okay?" I asked the golem. "What did you say to him?"

She said something else in the other language, too fast for me to pick individual words out of it even if I'd been able to understand them. Zaide spun on his heel like he was about to start marching, but instead he shuffled back toward his office area, where he sat down on the lounge he napped on. "Zaide?" I called after him, but he didn't even turn. It was like he didn't even realize he was a zaide.

The golem turned back to me. "He's fine," she said. She yawned. Could magical beings even get tired? "I just told him it was time for him to go take a nap."

It hadn't sounded like she'd been telling him to go take a nap. "It sounded kind of like what you were saying was mean," I said uncertainly.

Her eyes flashed in anger. "You've never seen me mean."

Her words were like a strong wind. I had to take a step back or they'd blow me over. "So you were actually telling him to go take a nap?"

"Would I lie to you?" she asked, which didn't help at all.

"Okay," I said, just as uncertainly as before. "I guess I believe you."

"Good." Her brilliant white teeth flashed in a smile. "Then go home. Dream of Isabella. I'll see you tomorrow."

Tomorrow dawned bright and clear. Zaide greeted me with a cheerful "Leah Roslyn!" and Matty had left her phone at home by mistake, which meant she had no choice but to pay attention to me. The golem was nowhere to be seen. It should have been a great afternoon.

Should have.

I felt haunted by what had happened yesterday. I tried to convince myself that I could trust the golem, that the golem wouldn't hurt Zaide or bully him around, but my brain wouldn't quite believe me. She'd been saying something mean, and then she'd lied to me about it.

Jed and Matty and I sat in the living area, cross-legged in a triangle on the floor. Jed was showing us some funny videos of guys messing up skateboard tricks—at least, he thought they were funny; I thought they mostly looked painful. "Hey," I said, after Jed laughed and I winced as a sorry kid nailed himself in the groin. "Have any of your friends ever lied to you? Or been mean to you?"

Jed set his phone down and swiveled to me, his eyes totally serious for once. "Tell me their name, and I will murder them."

Okay, that was not a great start. "I was looking for a, um, a less violent option," I said hastily. "Like maybe talking to them or something."

Matty slung an arm around my shoulders. "I only go to Jed when I want a dumb joke or him to beat someone up," she said. "For everything else, come to me. Who is this friend, and what did they say?"

Guilt trickled through me as I spoke, because this whole conversation was about how lying was bad, and yet here I was, bringing more lies into the world. I couldn't tell them the liar was Elsa, because what if I still needed her? "It's a girl at . . . school," I said. "I . . . found out she might have been saying some mean things about another friend behind her back, but she denied it."

"Is the other friend you?" Jed asked. He hit pause on the video. "I told you, I don't mind going to jail for you, Lee."

Matty rolled her eyes. "Ignore the idiot. Lee, if it were me, I'd ice her out. She knows what she did wrong." I couldn't exactly ice the golem out, though. Maybe that was good advice if I was talking to a real person. "Find some new friends, some real friends, because once someone's talking behind your back and lying to you, you're never going to trust them again. Or reconnect with your old friends. Don't you have really good friends at Schechter?"

I burst into tears.

"Oh no!" Matty said, her mouth forming an O of dismay. "What did I say?"

I wiped my eyes, trying to quiet down so that none of the adults would hear me, but it just turned into a nasty case of the hiccups. "My—*hic*—old—*hic*—friends . . ."

"Hold your breath and swallow six times—then the hiccups will go away," Jed said. I did, and they did. He glanced sidelong at Matty. "See, I can do things besides make dumb jokes and beat people up."

"Don't get ahead of yourself." Matty turned back to me. "What were you saying about your Schechter friends, Lee?"

"Everything's different. I feel like we're not really close anymore, and—and I'm *losing* them." Matty and Jed both knew friends. They had a ton of them. I wiped my face. "How can I make it so that I don't?"

"Well, you're keeping in touch with them, right? Talking about your lives and stuff?" Matty asked, her face pinched with sympathy. I nodded. "And you're getting together as much as you can?" I nodded again.

"Well, I think that's really all you can do, Lee," Jed said.

That couldn't be true. "There has to be more I can do," I said. "They're doing stuff without me all the time! And they're making a new friend I'm pretty sure is replacing me. I don't want them to forget me." I said the last part quietly. I was tired of people forgetting me.

They were silent for a moment. Then Matty said, "It doesn't sound like they're forgetting you. It just sounds like your friendship is changing."

"But I don't *want* it to change, Matty."

"How many times do I have to tell you I'm going by Matilda now?" She gave me the stink-eye. It was like a switch had gone off, and she was done giving good advice. She shrugged. "And tough luck. Everything changes."

Anger swelled in me like a wave. She was wrong. She had to be wrong. I'd tell her exactly how wrong she was, too, just as soon as I thought up a good response.

"Oh, don't get like that. I remember being your age," she said. She gave a world-weary sigh, like being thirteen was basically ancient. "I got a whole new group of friends going into eighth grade, when I started hanging out more with the other girls on the soccer team. It's not like I don't like my old friends anymore. They're still my friends. I just see the girls on the soccer team more often. A friendship where you're seeing someone every day is different from a friendship where you stay mostly in touch over the phone or online. But it doesn't make either of them any less real. Just different."

"Maybe," I said flatly. The anger was draining out of me. Now I just felt sad.

"You don't know how things are going to change," Matty continued. "What about when they graduate middle school? Aren't they going to go to public school? So even if you were still living there with them, you might be going to different high schools. Things would be changing anyway. You can't stop growing older."

"Unless you die," Jed pitched in.

Matty rolled her eyes.

It wasn't that I wanted to stop growing older. On the contrary—I'd be happy getting older faster. I couldn't wait to be able to drive. To work and earn my own money. To eat ice cream whenever I wanted. I just didn't want to lose my friends. "Thanks," I said.

Matty gave me a comforting pat on the shoulder. "It's going to be okay. I promise. Being the new kid is hard, but eventually you'll find your people."

Right. Maybe if Isabella Lynch could become my friend and I could be popular and fit in, this would all be worth it. "That's true," I said, and hoped Matty wouldn't ask any more questions.

"Good," Jed said, and then he roared, "Let's hug it out!" He dove over us, knocking us up against the hard floor. And even though I thought my shoulder blades would probably be bruised later, it was worth it.

CHAPTER TWELVE

I WOULDN'T HAVE BELIEVED IT if you'd told me
a few days earlier, but I actually forgot about Isabella's
invitation until Sunday morning. I blinked into the
fuzzy sunlight filtering through my curtains and wondered what time it was.

The sound of clanging pots and pans and knives
met me as I drifted down the stairs. I perked up. That
sounded like a big, fancy breakfast. French toast? Pan-
cakes? Waffles? My stomach let out a ferocious growl.
Like there was an actual big cat growling behind me, I
hopped down the stairs and skidded into the kitchen.

Where there was definitely no French toast or pan-
cakes or waffles.

My shoulders slumped in disappointment as I took in what was *actually* going on. The counter was heaped with boxes and bags of walnuts, figs, prunes, dried dates, and dried apricots. Apples scattered around like they were trying to run away from the gleaming silver apple corer. There were opened boxes of matzah, their contents soaking in a pan of yellowy-white gloop.

"Good morning," my mom said from behind me, holding a massive knife. That sounded like the beginning of a nightmare, and if you considered this breakfast disappointment a nightmare—as I did—it held up.

"No breakfast?" I asked. Hope rose in my voice. It could still happen. I was sure we had all the necessary ingredients. "French toast?"

My mom shook her head, sweeping past me. She set the giant knife down on the counter with a clink. "Seder prep for Passover."

"When's the seder?" It was weird, not knowing when it was. In Jewish school, we'd discuss the holidays and calendar all the time. But since practically no one else in my new school was Jewish, the holidays felt like they snuck up on me. Like a few weeks ago, with Purim. It totally snuck up behind me, and I didn't see it until it was too late. *Boom! It's Purim! Have you decided on your costume yet?*

When I went to Schechter, we'd start thinking about our Purim costumes ages in advance, practically as soon as Chanukah ended, even though Purim didn't usually come around till March-ish. When I was a little girl, all my friends and I would go as the Purim heroine, Queen Esther, but we changed it up as we got older. Last year, Lexy and Julie and I went as our Hebrew school teachers. Julie got particularly inspired when it came to imitating Rabbi Paskind's beard.

This year I went as nothing. Why bother? Even though the Purim carnival at our old temple was on a Sunday, Mom and Dad were busy and couldn't do the two-hour trip.

"The first night is Monday," Mom said, and the word *Monday* was like a lightning bolt direct to my brain.

"Oh! I'm supposed to go over to Isabella Lynch's house on Monday after school."

I said Isabella's name the way we'd say Queen Esther's name when reading the Purim story, but the effect was lost on my mom. "You'll have to reschedule then," she said. "We're due at Zaide's at four."

School was over at 2:27. "I could still go to Isabella's

for a half hour . . . ," I said, but my heart wasn't even in it. It wouldn't make sense for me to go all the way to Isabella's for a mere half hour, and my mom wasn't going to drive all the way out there to pick me up when she had to make half the seder food.

"No."

"Fine," I said. Hopefully Isabella's invitation would extend until Thursday or Friday. Maybe it would even make me look cooler, saying I had to reschedule. Like I could possibly have something better to do than going over to Isabella's house.

"Leah." Mom's voice broke through my thoughts. "Would you help me chop the fruit and nuts for the charoset, please?" She pronounced the first syllable of *charoset* like she was clearing her throat. The *chhh* sound in Hebrew was one of my favorites to make. The boys in my old class used to say it like they were hacking up a big wad of spit in their throats. "I want to get started on the matzah ball soup."

"Sure." I hadn't had breakfast, but I could make my own breakfast by sampling all the charoset ingredients: the apples, the dates, the figs and prunes, the apricots, the walnuts. They weren't quite as good as French toast, but they were passable. And then I had a spark of life-changing inspiration. "Hey," I said, grabbing the smallest knife I could find. "You know what would be amazing? *Charoset French toast.*"

I waited for my mom's face to break open in awe, but she just kept mixing and measuring. "Mom?" I prompted.

"Leah," she said. "I've been meaning to talk to you."

I focused on the fruit. Chopping apples was easy, but chopping the dates and apricots and figs and prunes was hard. They were sticky and mushy and liked to cling not just to one another but to the knife. I always felt kind of bad for them, like they were fighting for their lives. "Okay. What?"

She sighed. "I know you've been struggling lately. I've wanted to talk to you about it, but things have been so busy with Zaide and with the new job, and—"

"I'm not struggling," I said. Had she overheard my talk with Matty and Jed? Well, Naomi might have stolen my friends from me, but I still had plans to go over to Isabella Lynch's house, for heaven's sake.

"I mean with Zaide," she replied. "I went through the same thing with my great-grandmother. Zaide's mother. I was nine when she died."

My knife slammed into the cutting board, separating

the woody stem of a fig from its seedy flesh. It ably hard enough and sharp enough to cut o if I missed. "Zaide's not dead," I said, not looking up.

My mom kept on talking like I hadn't just made an important point. "Bubbe Anna was eighty-nine years old. Fit as a fiddle in body. It was her mind that started to go near the end. She started forgetting my name, or thinking I was my mother or grandmother or a stranger."

She took a deep breath. The spongy sounds of her mixing stopped. I was tempted to look over in support in case she was upset, but I had a lot of things to chop. And my hands were sticky. And also if I looked at her, I might cry.

"She passed away before my parents could talk about moving her somewhere that would be safer for her," Mom continued. Her voice was lower now. Yeah, she was definitely trying not to cry. I blinked hard to keep my cutting board from going blurry. I definitely did not want to miss with my knife. "It was very hard. I loved my bubbe."

She paused. I knew she was waiting for me to say something, maybe acknowledge that we were in similar situations, but we weren't. So I just kept chopping and swiping my pile of fruit and nuts to the side. Chopping and swiping. Chop and swipe.

Mom sighed again. "Leah, Zaide is in the beginning stages of Alzheimer's disease. Have you heard of Alzheimer's?"

I shrugged. I had heard of Alzheimer's—Julie's grandfather had it. But I let my mom explain it anyway. Maybe then she'd have to admit that Zaide didn't have it.

"Someone who has Alzheimer's starts out by forgetting little things," Mom said. "Then bigger things. Names, places. They can get confused easily. They might go to the grocery store and get disoriented and panic, or they might go out for a walk, forget where they are, and wander into the street."

That didn't sound like Zaide. And even if it did, that was why I kept the golem around. As long as she did her job, Zaide wouldn't panic at the grocery store or wander into the street and get hit by a car.

Mom was busy saying something about how he needed supervision and that the nursing home they were looking at was actually a pretty nice place, which was obviously a lie. "We all need to be on the same side in this, Leah," she finished. When she said your name a lot, that's when you knew she was serious.

But I could be serious, too. "I'm on Zaide's side."

If she kept sighing like this, she was going to fill the entire room up with carbon dioxide, and we were going to suffocate to death. "The only reason we haven't moved Zaide yet is because he refuses to go anywhere," she said. "But he can only do that for so long. We're going to take him to the doctor, Leah." My name again. "Leah . . ." Double name. *Extra* serious. "Please understand that we're not trying to hurt Zaide or hide him away somewhere. This is for his own good. The facility is very close by, we can still visit him whenever we—"

"But it's not on the same block. I thought that was why we moved here in the whole frigging place."

"I don't appreciate your language, Leah." I hacked through an entire apple, imagining that if I chopped hard enough I could stop this entire conversation from happening. "And yes, we did move here to be closer to Zaide. Which was good because your father and I hadn't realized how bad it had gotten. I'm glad we're here to take care of him." Her voice wavered a bit. "You know, he and Bubbe Ruth were more parents to me than grandparents."

I did know that. My mom's parents, my grandparents, had died in a car crash when she was fifteen. She and

Uncle Marvin had been adopted by Zaide and Bubbe Ruth.

"But still," I said. "We could just have him move in here. It's easy. He can just—"

"It's not easy, Leah!"

I jumped at the snap in my mom's voice—bad idea while you're holding a knife. I faced away from her, curling into myself.

When she spoke again, her voice was softer. "I'm sorry for snapping at you. But you have to understand: None of this is easy. I've been spending hours every day with Zaide or working on plans for his care. Work is getting so busy, and I haven't gotten to spend as much time with you as I want. If he moved in here, keeping him safe would be a full-time job, one I'm not trained for. Do you understand?"

I knew that if I said no, she'd get upset. So even though I thought—no, *knew*—that she was wrong, I said, "Yes."

"Good." Her footsteps creaked on the floor, got louder. She was coming closer. "Wow, Leah!" A hand landed on my shoulder and squeezed. "I think you've chopped enough for *three* Passovers. You can stop!"

I blinked down at the cutting board. She was right.

All the fruits and nuts I'd chopped were overflowing the wood surface and spilling off onto the counter. I set the knife down. Took a bow.

She laughed. A small laugh, but a laugh nonetheless. It made me feel good. "You know what? Let's take the extra and use up our bread before Passover as well. Charoset French toast it is."

I was right about two things: We needed the golem, and charoset French toast *was* delicious.

CHAPTER THIRTEEN

BY THE TIME I RETURNED to school on Monday, last Friday's lunch seemed almost like a dream. Maybe it *had* been a dream. And when I told Isabella that I couldn't go over to her house today, she would cock her head and squint like she was trying to remember what my name was.

No, it'd be worse. I imagined what would happen when I walked into the cafeteria: I'd move to sit at her *table*, and Isabella would cock her head and squint like an alien was trying to sit there.

So I was paralyzed with dread. I stood outside the crush of the kids trying to get into the lunchroom, pretending to flip through my folder so I didn't have to go inside. I didn't want to take the chance of missing out with Isabella, but I also couldn't handle the withering humiliation of going over there, being turned away by Isabella and her friends, and then having to slink back to the Three Ds, all three of whom would be looking at me with immense pity.

I jumped when an arm slung itself over my shoulder. "Leah!" someone said into my ear. I leaned away, disliking the feel of people's warm, moist breath tickling my ear. But I realized belatedly that this person's breath was none of that. It was dry as stone.

I pulled back to find the golem standing there. I didn't think I'd ever been this close to her before . . . well, outside the night I'd built that little body of dirt and mud. Her skin was so smooth—I didn't see a single pore. It was like a doll's plastic coating.

"Hello, Elsa," I said. I waited for her to pull back, but she didn't move. Those nearly gold eyes regarded me calmly.

"Hello, Leah."

Most human beings have striations in their eyes. Blue eyes aren't entirely blue; Matty and Jed have streaks of green and brown and gold. My own eyes look totally dark brown from far away, but when I look at them up close in the mirror, they have little splotches of light brown and green and even some yellow, which is cool, and when I was little, I thought it made me part cat. (My mom dashed those hopes quickly.) The golem's eyes had none of that. They were a pure, unchanging brown gold.

"Are you coming?" the golem asked.

Something made me hesitate. Maybe it was the look in her eyes. Or to be more specific, the absence of one. No kindness and no malice. I had no idea whether she was being genuine or planning something cruel. I didn't know why I was thinking it right now, but I imagined her sitting down at Isabella's table and looking up and laughing that there was no room for me.

"I guess." Because whether I trusted her or not, I'd made her. I deserved whatever was coming.

The cafeteria was bustling, as usual. Most kids were either already seated or lined up near the kitchens at the far wall waiting for their food. The Three Ds brought lunch every day like I did, so they were already at their table. My eyes landed on them out of habit, and my heart fluttered. The three of them were staring at me unblinkingly, like one of those scenes in the movies where people turn into zombies and they're about to dive on you and eat you. In an attempt to break the awkwardness, I waved in their direction. They didn't wave back. Just stared.

I nearly collapsed in relief when we got close to Isabella's table and I realized that the same two spaces had been cleared on the bench. Still, I didn't whoosh out all the worry until we'd actually sat down and nobody shouted at me to go away.

Instead, Isabella actually turned to me and smiled. "Hey, Leah." She'd gotten my name right! "Today still on?"

Okay, Leah. You can make it through this conversation without saying anything stupid. "I actually can't today," I said. I tried to make it sound like an apology. "Or tomorrow. Maybe another day this week?"

I'd as good as told her that I had better things to do than hang out with her, so I expected her to counter. To say that another day this week didn't work because of course she also had better things to do than hang out with me, but maybe some other time?

Instead, she nodded. "Friday works for me!" she exclaimed. The other kids around us, including the golem, were silent. I couldn't read any expressions on their faces. Maybe the Three Ds had actually turned into zombies, and now these kids were all turning, too. "I have a student government makeup day from when we had those snow days. You'll take the late bus home with me."

I nodded along. It hadn't been a question.

"Okay, cool," Isabella said. She clapped her hands together. "What should we do? Maybe we should do each other's hair! Let me see your hair."

Again, it wasn't a request. Before I could even bow my head, her hands were tangled in my curls. I swallowed back a cry of pain at the pulling and just bowed my head farther, giving her easier access. I had no idea what she was looking for, but her hands explored all the way over my head, practically giving me a scalp massage. It felt weird.

Her hands lingered on my head for one last second before pulling away. I lifted my head. My whole scalp tingled now. I was pretty sure my curls were messed up, too. You can't really comb your hands through curly hair without it becoming a big mass of staticky frizz. But that was okay. Isabella's hands had made it a big mass of staticky frizz, so it was basically a badge of honor. A signal that I'd been chosen.

Isabella pursed her lips. For some reason, she looked

disappointed. I had no idea why. She could see what my hair looked like from the other side of the cafeteria. It wasn't like touching it was going to tell her anything new or exciting.

I had to break the awkward silence. "Hair sounds good!" For some ungodly reason, I pumped my fist in the air. Then I immediately regretted it. My cheeks began to burn.

Elsa saved me. She clapped me on the back so hard she nearly sent my forehead thudding into the table. "That reminds me of the time I was in Paris and I had my hair done by Alfonse de Shampoo, the world's greatest hairstylist!" she said. "His great-great-grandfather was the inventor of shampoo. He named it after himself. Isn't that grand?"

I had no idea what to say to that. I was 99 percent sure the golem was making that fact up entirely, much less the man. Then again, maybe her specific grains of dirt had been made into golems before, and one had lived in France. They'd been floating around in synagogues for hundreds of years. Who's to say that Zaide was the first person to find them?

The golem went on, babbling about how Alfonse de Shampoo had woven her hair—waist length at the time—

with crystals and heaped it so high on her head she had to duck to go through doorways. I fought back the urge to ask her if Alfonse de Shampoo was married to Luc de Conditioner, and instead I propped my chin up on my hand and snuck a glance backward at the Three Ds.

They weren't looking at me. I couldn't decide how I felt about that. Happy, I figured. I was happy they weren't thinking about me anymore. It meant they also weren't laughing at me, at how I once thought I could be a part of their group.

Those thoughts darkened my mind enough that I didn't do much else for the rest of lunch but laugh along with whatever jokes Isabella made and pretend to believe the golem's stories. When we all got up to leave for class, a hand like an iron shackle closed around my upper arm. Without straining against it, I knew I couldn't have moved if I tried.

"Leah," Elsa said. "I need to talk to you for a second."

It didn't seem like I had a choice. I let the rest of Isabella's group vanish into the ether of the hallway. Then I let the golem pull me behind a quiet stand of lockers. "What is it?" I asked.

"I want to spend more time with my new friends and less time at the old man's house," she said. She didn't move or giggle or twist a strand of hair around her finger the way she had while telling her fanciful stories at the lunch table. Just stared me down from her higher height. "I enjoy being popular and surrounded by adoring people fawning over me and my stories. Not so much cleaning after your zaide and keeping him from running out into the street."

I didn't even have to think. I just shook my head. The whole reason I'd created her was to look after Zaide, and I thought I was being pretty nice, actually, by letting her spend some time away from him. "Sorry."

Something dark flashed over her face, but it cleared. She knew she couldn't do anything without my permission. "Okay. I would like to ask you something else."

"What is it?"

"I want to come to your family's seder," she said.

"Why?" Lexy had come to my family's seder one year because her dad had gotten sick and they couldn't host, so it wasn't like I hadn't ever brought guests to a seder before. If I asked my parents if I could bring a friend, they would say yes.

I just wasn't sure I wanted to. Though it would be a nice thing to do after telling her she couldn't have what she really wanted . . .

She smiled at me. All of her teeth looked pointed. I blinked in surprise, then looked closer. Her teeth all looked normal. I must have been seeing things. "I've been listening to the old man talk about it for days," she said. "Do you know he talks to his dead wife when he thinks no one's listening? When he's in his right mind, too. Does he think she's listening down from heaven?"

Hearing that made me heavily, impossibly sad, a weight dragging me down. So I chose not to yell at her for being insensitive but to focus on the factual inaccuracy, which made some of the sadness disappear. "We don't have a heaven in Judaism, so probably not," I said. "Maybe he just likes to pretend she's still there. They were married for, like, a million years. It's probably hard for him to be alone."

Maybe it would be good for him to be around a bunch of other old people if the assisted-living facility is nice, some traitorous part of my mind whispered. I shut it down quickly.

"Anyway, from all he's been saying about it, it sounds fun," she said. "And he said it might be the last one. So I want to make sure I get in on it."

He was saying it might be the last one? Okay, I wasn't just shutting that traitorous part of my brain down, I was expelling it. Next time I blew my nose, it was coming out.

I couldn't let this be the last seder Zaide ever hosted. I wouldn't. Where would we go instead? We couldn't all fit in our dining room, or Matty and Jed's dining room. And where would the out-of-town cousins stay?

It didn't make any sense.

"Leah?" the golem said sharply, and when I looked back at her, her eyes were black. I took a step back and closed my eyes, willing them to turn back to their usual brown gold when I opened them, but . . . no. They stayed black. Black all the way through, no whites at all, dull and hard. Like someone had scooped her eyeballs out when I wasn't looking and replaced them with stones. Those eyes focused on me, and it was like they could see under my skin, and my insides curdled, and I had to make them stop, and—"Fine," I said. I closed my eyes a little bit too long. This time, when I opened them, hers stared back clear and calm and golden brown. I sucked in a deep breath and wiped my sweaty palms on my jeans.

"Good," she said sweetly, turning to go. "I'll get back to the old man now. Can't wait for tonight!"

The feeling those eyes gave me stuck around for the rest of the day. A cold, sticky, heavy feeling.

I couldn't help but wonder if this was what foreboding felt like.

CHAPTER FOURTEEN

WHATEVER IT WAS, THAT CREEPING feeling wore off by that evening. The seder left nothing but excitement behind. Excitement that wasn't even dampened when Elsa showed up at our door holding a box of jelly rings. "I found these in the Passover section of the store, so my mom said I should bring them," she said. She smiled up at my parents, revealing a pair of deep dimples in her cheeks, so deep I couldn't see the bottom. Had she always had dimples?

"Thank you, sweetie." My mom took the box of jelly rings from her. "These are Leah's father's favorite."

My favorite Passover dessert, too, though, to be fair, since you couldn't use flour in Passover desserts, a favorite

Passover dessert was like a favorite rainy-day beach. How could you go wrong with firm rings of tart jelly coated with chocolate, though? Or anything coated in chocolate, really?

We walked over together, carefully carrying the casserole dishes and giant bowls half the meal was in. Mom and Dad had to go back to carry the rest, but there wasn't enough for me and Elsa to do a second round, so we stayed behind. The first ones there.

I eyed Zaide carefully. "Zaide, you remember my friend Elsa, right?" This was a dangerous game. I had no idea if clearheaded Zaide was aware that someone had been living with him, keeping him safe. If he'd spotted her hair under the bed.

Zaide flashed the golem a toothless smile. "Elsa, it is good to see you." He didn't call her Maria. He didn't panic. He acted like he was seeing my old friend Lexy at that past seder.

I let my shoulders relax. This would be fine. This would all be fine. "Elsa moved in recently down the street," I said. "She's not Jewish, but I told her about Passover, and she was interested in checking out the seder."

"You are always welcome," Zaide told her. "Any stranger is welcome at our table on Passover."

"Like Elijah," I said, and he laughed. We were supposed to crack the door on Passover for the prophet Elijah to come by and drink the goblet of wine left for him on the table. I wasn't quite clear if Elijah was supposed to be a ghost or a skeleton or what. When Matty and Jed and I were little, we always got gape-mouthed in awe at how Elijah's glass was empty by the end of the night. A couple of years later we realized that Zaide was the one who drank it. What a betrayal.

"You can help set the table," he said to me. "Just be careful with the good china. Don't drop anything." I nodded to show I understood, then Elsa trooped along with me to the kitchen, where we piled our arms full of plates and silverware. Mom always argued that we should use paper plates because it would be so much easier to clean up, but Zaide was firm about using the good china. He said it didn't feel like a holiday without the good china.

At the table, we put them down and then dragged out all the kitchen chairs, shoving them together as tight as they'd go. We'd probably need a few of the folding chairs from the garage as well. We needed enough room for my parents and me, plus Elsa, plus Uncle Marvin and Aunt Jessie and Matty and Jed, plus the assorted faraway cousins trekking all the way here. And Zaide, of course, in the grand chair in the middle. He didn't like sitting at the head of the table—he said he felt too distant from the action.

"I don't get this table," Elsa said to me, leaning over the dining table. "I mean, why do you want to eat on a picture of your face?"

I glanced automatically at Zaide to see if he'd overheard and was insulted, but of course he hadn't been able to hear her. "I love this table," I said. It was long and wooden with a glass top, and beneath the glass surface were arrayed photographs of our family. My mom and Uncle Marvin as little kids splashing in a wading pool. Me and Matty and Jed from a few years ago in our temple best before a faraway cousin's bat mitzvah. My grandma who I hadn't ever met, on her wedding day, the photo browning, its edges ragged. It was like taking a tour through the lives of Zaide's descendants.

Elsa scoffed. "I think it's weird."

"You can think whatever you want." I handed her a few plates to set down at the far end of the table while I arranged them on this end. I paused a moment to admire the photo below me before I covered it up. It was me and Matty and Jed from not all that long ago; Zaide had slipped this photo between the glass when I asked him why the photos stopped when we were little. It was a Yom Kippur, when we fasted, and I remembered we'd all been starving (even if Jed had snuck a few granola bars in the bathroom), but we were beaming cheek to cheek anyway.

"Family is a strange thing," Elsa said from the other end of the table. I looked over to find her examining the photos beneath her, as well. "It's like you're stuck with these other people, and whether you like them or not, whether you fit in with them or not, it doesn't matter."

"I guess that's one way of putting it."

Elsa squinted down at the photo. I couldn't see it from where I was standing, but I knew from having memorized the entire table which one she was looking at. It was Zaide and Bubbe Ruth with my grandma and my mom and Uncle Marvin when they were little. The group of them were at some kind of fair, my tiny mom stuffing her face with cotton candy and Uncle Marvin looking longingly at my grandma's funnel cake. "The different level of bonds are very interesting. Is the bond between you and your great-grandfather the same as the one between you and your mother, or the ones between you and your cousins?"

I set another plate down. It clinked on the glass surface. "I don't know. Like, people don't think of it that way."

"Interesting." She cocked her head, still staring at the photo. "I wonder what it would take to destroy them."

"Yeah." I set another plate down. Then her words caught up to my brain. "Wait, what?"

I glanced up in time to see a plate fall from her hands. *The good china!* I dove for it, but it was futile, and I knew it even as my knees smashed up against the hard floor. The plate smashed up against the hard floor, too, breaking cleanly in two.

"What was that?"

I climbed to my feet as Zaide shuffled over. I winced. "Elsa dropped a plate," I said. I waited for the golem to apologize, but she was silent. She was looking back and forth between me and Zaide, head cocked as if she were waiting for something to happen. "She's very sorry."

Zaide tutted in disapproval. "Make sure to clean it up so that nobody steps on it." He leaned in toward me and whispered, so Elsa couldn't hear. "Do you know how many plates of the good china your mother broke as a child?" He tutted. "It was like she was trying to juggle them."

I cracked a little smile. He smiled back, his mismatched teeth on full display, then shuffled back toward the kitchen.

"He loves those plates, but not as much as he loves you or your mother," the golem mused as I cleaned up the plate. "Interesting."

I gave her a sidelong glance. I'd assumed her dropping the plate had been an accident.

Now I wasn't so sure.

This could be bad.

After setting the table, I got to prepare the seder plate. It was technically ready in the fridge, covered with a tight sheen of plastic wrap, but I unwrapped it and brought it to the dining area. I loved our family seder plate as much as the table. It was blue and white with diamond-like designs and was one of the few things Zaide's parents had been able to bring over from the old country. Many of the designs were hidden right now by the traditional occupants of the seder plate, all of which represented some aspect of our people or the Passover story: the hard-boiled egg, the horseradish, the shank bone Mom had picked up from the butcher, some of the charoset we'd made before, and some celery. I crowned it with a small stack of matzah once it was sitting proudly in the center of the table, right in front of Zaide.

"That brown bone looks gross," the golem said over my shoulder. "And horseradish and egg? Yuck."

"Don't go near it," I warned.

She tried to step around me and—big surprise—go near it, but I blocked her. She tried to step around me again, and I moved with her. "Why did you even want to come?" I hissed.

She smiled at me and didn't answer. I was ready to scream when the door opened behind us. Mom and Dad were back with the rest of the meal, and then Matty and Jed and my aunt and uncle were filing through with their own dishes and trays and pots. After them, the faraway cousins came pouring through the door, and I was kissing the cheeks of people I saw only once a year. Then we were all sitting down, me between Elsa and Jed on the far side of the table. Matty claimed the seat on Elsa's other side and had her wrapped up in a conversation about soccer before I could ask Elsa if she wanted to switch seats.

There are two truths about the Passover seder that seem contradictory yet somehow exist at the same time: I love it . . . and it's incredibly boring. Like, *zzzzz* on-the-table-within-fifteen-minutes boring, where you wake up fifteen minutes later to find that you're not even close to halfway through. Everybody reads paragraphs from the Haggadah—the book that tells the story of Passover—in Hebrew, so I can't understand what we're saying. I don't even get to sing the Four Questions anymore, since the honor goes to the youngest person at the table, and seven-year-old faraway cousin Sammy is old enough to do them now. If I try to talk to Jed or Matty, we get a *look* from Zaide. I know. The man's half-deaf, and yet he seems to have sonar for seder whispering.

Elsa behaved herself through the seder, which was fortunate. After what felt like a thousand years, we finally got to eat the festive meal. I hopped up—my legs were stiff after sitting so long—and helped the others bring in first the gefilte fish, then the sliced egg in salt water, then the matzah ball soup. We passed the bowls around, and then, finally, finally, I got to sit down and—

"I'd like to make a speech," Zaide announced.

This was not part of the usual routine. I laid my spoon down, suppressing a groan. I just wanted to eat my soft, delicious matzah ball and the mushy carrots cooked with it.

Zaide pushed himself to a standing position, his hands pressed on the table before him. My mom and Uncle Marvin looked up at him from their places at his right and left. "We all know the Passover story," Zaide said. "The story of our ancestors' narrow escape from ancient Egypt, where they were slaves. We've gone from slaves toiling away in the hot sands to free people here in this comfortable house at this comfortable table with our safe, healthy loved ones.

"It makes me so happy to see all of you here. My family. Just the fact that all of us can gather here freely and perform this tradition year after year is how I tell the ancient Egyptians and the Nazis and all of the other people who wanted—and want—us dead that we won. That they are gone and we are still here. That we will never die. *Am Yisrael chai.*"

The people of Israel live. As in ancient Israel, where the Jewish people came from. Aka, the Jewish people live. I gave Mom and Dad a smug look. That little speech was basically Zaide saying that as long as he was here in his house hosting the Passover seder, the Nazis would know they'd lost. How could you argue with that?

The golem gave a little cough beside me, one almost too quiet to hear. But if she hadn't meant for me to hear it, I wouldn't have heard it, considering she didn't have the need to fulfill basic biological functions like coughing. She must have been trying to get my attention, but I didn't let on. I didn't want to hear whatever obnoxious comment she was going to make about the speech. Or even imagine the possibilities.

"This may be my last year hosting the seder," Zaide continued, and I nodded along before realizing, *Wait, what?* "But it doesn't matter where we are or who is in charge. Even what Haggadah you use, or if you decide to shorten the ceremony a bit. Though I'll be glaring down at you—whether Jews actually have a heaven or not." He gave my dad a stern look, and my dad laughed—he tried to get us to skip half the service every year. "As long as you're all here every year, you'll be fulfilling my promise. Fulfilling the tradition. I'd like to propose a toast, to us. To our family."

He went to raise his wineglass, but I raised my whole body, which made his glass stop in the middle. I took a deep breath. Even though this was family, I didn't like talking in front of so many people at once. But I had to. Because clearly Mom and Dad and Uncle Marvin had been weakening his defenses. He was beginning to fold, and he didn't want to. He needed my help.

"I would just like to add . . ." My body was all tingly with nerves, so I stopped to take another deep breath, which should hopefully chase some of those nerves out. It didn't work. "I would just like to add that this tradition is very important to me, too. Specifically, this place, this house, with *all* of you. Even the cousins I only see once a year. Who probably wouldn't come if it weren't for Zaide being here." I shot my mom a quick look. She wasn't giving me the angry glare I was expecting, the one for interfering with all of her cajoling and convincing.

The look she was giving me was actually kind of . . . sad.

I shook that look right off and continued, my words spilling out in a rush. The sooner they were out, the sooner I could sit back down and escape all these eyes on me. "Zaide is the one person in our family who actually escaped the Nazis, so his presence is what shows the world that we're still here. That *am Yisrael chai*. Basically, if Zaide is not here in this repurposed telephone company building, the Nazis win." I raised my own glass of grape juice. "To Zaide and this house!"

Silence. Everybody blinked at me. It took a moment for people to begin raising their glasses. I sat myself back down, relief whooshing over me. I'd done it. I'd done my part. No way Mom and Dad could think about stashing Zaide away after that speech.

Before the glasses touched anybody's lips, a tinging sounded. The tinging of somebody clanking their spoon on their wineglass.

Or grape-juice glass. The golem stood. Everybody's glasses hung in midair, like they were unsure what they were supposed to be doing right about now.

"I would also like to make a speech," the golem announced. From my position below her, I could see the underside of her chin. A shadow. I squinted. No, that wasn't a shadow. A good square inch beneath her chin was solid packed dirt.

I didn't have time to think about that now, though. Not while that square inch of dirt was moving up and down with her jaw as she spoke.

"I am not Jewish, but my best friend Leah kindly invited me to your gathering today," she said. Her voice still had the tone of an announcement. Matty caught my eye behind the golem's back and mouthed, *Best friend?* When I shrugged in response, she scowled. It actually felt kind of good to see her unhappy about that, like she was telling me she was supposed to be my best friend. "I've moved all over the world with my parents, and we haven't had any sort of traditions like this. It's wonderful to see all of you coming together like this. A beautiful thing."

She tilted her head. "And I have to say, Leah, that you were wrong. Leah told me I might not want to attend tonight because of how terrible her relatives are." I stiffened. What was she doing?

"She told me that her cousins were stupid and boring, especially Jed, who can't even pass math, and that her parents were annoying and embarrassing to be around," the golem proclaimed, lifting her glass high. "And she said she couldn't wait for her great-grandfather to die, because she was sick of how old and gross he was. But I have to say, none of that is true. You all seem like very nice people."

"None of that is true. I didn't say any of that," I said, but from the heat climbing on my cheeks and the galloping of my heart, it had to look like I was lying.

"A toast!" the golem proclaimed. Nobody lifted their glasses in unison with her, only looked at me with wide eyes.

"Did you really say that?" Jed asked. I could see all the white around his pupils. He looked hurt. Matty did, too, her head drooping over the table.

They cared what I thought of them. They weren't ready to ditch me for the nearest soccer team.

That thought motivated me enough to stand up again. "I did not say any of that. I don't know if Elsa is mistaken or lying, but none of that came from me." I sat back down.

Still nobody toasted. People kept staring at me, and I kept staring back, my face flaming, until the murmur of conversation rose around the table, and then people started eating, and I sank back into my chair.

"That was interesting," Elsa mused.

"Why would you say all of that?" I hissed at her. "You know none of that was true!"

She shrugged. "You brought it upon yourself, Leah." *What? How?* And then I remembered. At school. When I'd told her she couldn't be a popular girl full-time, because she had a job to do here.

She was punishing me.

Before I could say anything, she stood. "I'm going to go to the bathroom." Only she walked toward the front door, and then out the front door, and she was gone.

Matty shifted over into the golem's seat. "She said you brought it upon yourself? So she basically admitted she was lying." She shook her head, her lip curling in disgust. "What a little witch. She'd better have gone home."

"I think she did," I said. I had no idea where she'd gone. "Wait, you thought there was a possibility she *wasn't* lying?"

"It's not that," Matty said, though her face drooped with apology. "It's just that . . . I . . ." She shook her head. "Never mind. Let's not talk about it."

"Leah." Jed talked over her from my other side. "Hey, Leah. Are you ready?"

I would let Matty off the hook. For now. I turned to Jed, pasting a smile on my face. "Always," I said. "But for what?"

"The mushy carrots!"

Before I could react, he smashed one of the mushy carrots from his soup into my hand. I squealed and tried to pull away, but it was too late. I had a fistful of mashed carrot.

It was tradition. He had to.

I shook my hand, sending about half of the smushy vegetable bits to the floor. But I didn't have any time to waste. "Think fast!"

I also had to. It was tradition.

Jed did not think fast. Not fast enough, anyway, to

avoid the rest of the mushy carrot from splattering in his own hand. "Eww," he laughed as he shook it off onto the floor. It landed with a splat on the rug.

For some reason, my mom was not as into this tradition as Jed and I were.

We leaned over as if to survey the damage. Our foreheads nearly knocked together. In a whisper, he asked, "Is everything okay with your friend?"

She's not really my friend is what I wanted to say. *She's not really a person* is what I wanted to say next. But I didn't say any of that. Instead I shrugged.

This was the first time I'd kept a secret from Matty and Jed. It felt weird. Weird bad.

I wished I didn't need the golem. Then I could just rip her stupid papery tongue out of her mouth and put her pile of dirt back into the envelope for the next sucker. But I did need her. Without her, Zaide would probably already be locked away in the nursing home.

"I have to talk to her, but it'll be okay," I said. "How about you?" I definitely hadn't imagined the hurt look that had crossed his face when the golem said he was failing math.

"I'm about average," he said. "Zaide's really been helping." Which was why this couldn't be our last seder. I couldn't let my cousin fail math and repeat the same grade over and over and over. This was all for Jed as much as it was for me. I ignored the little voice in the back of my head that said otherwise.

When we went to sit back up, our foreheads did bang. For a second before the pain set in, I actually saw stars.

CHAPTER FIFTEEN

THE REST OF THE SEDER passed in a blur of awkward laughter and *How's school?*s. For the first time ever, I was happy when it ended. I cornered both of my parents and Zaide, who assured me that they knew the golem had been lying. I was happier still knowing that a couple of the faraway cousins would be staying with Zaide and keeping an eye on him and the golem, if she was there, too.

The second night of Passover was smaller—just me and my parents at our house. Zaide liked to have some time to catch up with the faraway cousins he saw only once or twice a year, and Matty and Jed had some school thing they had to do. At least I got to sing the Four Questions.

By the time Friday rolled around, I was thrumming with excitement for my afternoon at Isabella's house. I stood in front of my closet and dismissed one outfit after another. Most of them were fine for school, but for undergoing the scrutiny of extra time with Isabella at her surely very fashionable home? Probably not. I finally settled upon dark distressed jeans with one of my dad's old band T-shirts on top. The great thing about this shirt was that it looked okay worn normally to fool any teachers intent on enforcing the school's dress code (no bare shoulders, young lady!) but actually looked even better slipping off one shoulder and revealing a hint of one scandalous bra strap. I turned a few angles in my full-length mirror and gave myself a decisive nod. Isabella would approve.

I met up with Isabella in the school courtyard after a chorus practice for me and a makeup student government meeting for her. I wasn't even nervous, since chorus had wrung all the nervousness out of me. That was one of the reasons I liked it. That, and it reminded me of my old school. We spent a lot of time at Jewish school singing prayers and the Shabbat services as a group and with solos. Singing to me felt purifying, calming. I certainly wasn't the best singer at school and harbored no pipe dreams about "making it big" or whatever, but I had fun.

Isabella did not have the same attitude about student government. She rolled her eyes at me as she jogged over, her satchel—much cooler than a backpack—bouncing heavily against her side. "I hate student government," she said breathlessly, slowing in front of me. She didn't even say hi, or give me one of those half-hearted half hugs. "But it's going to look so good on my résumé when I run for student government in high school, which I'll need for student government in college, which I'll need when I run for real office when I'm grown-up."

I didn't get it. "If you hate it, why do you want to keep doing it?"

She blinked at me twice, bowing her head a little and looking up at me like I'd said something stupid. "*Because* I'm going to be president when I'm thirty-five, so I need a lot of experience."

"Oh."

She tossed her hair over her shoulder. "And I'll definitely like being president. Who wouldn't?"

I didn't think I'd like being president. It sounded really stressful. One of my teachers last year would show us pictures of presidents on their first day of office and on their last day of office four or eight years later. All of them looked like they'd aged at least thirty years. Much grayer hair, more wrinkles on their faces. A sad look in their eyes.

But maybe Isabella was different. "You'd make a good president," I said dutifully, even though I wasn't really sure if that was true. If the point of a president was to model fashion sense before an entire nation, it was definitely true. Today she was wearing a sleeveless flowered sundress that would have looked out of place for chilly early April if it hadn't been worn over a black turtleneck with some metallic silver leggings underneath. It made for a neat clash of nature and industrial chic.

She flashed a smile at me. She had a great president smile, that was true, too. One of those smiles that drew people to her, made you want to listen to whatever she said. "Thanks," Isabella said. "What do you want to be? You should really be planning now so that you can take all the right classes and do all the right activities."

Me? I had no idea. My parents were always telling me that I didn't have to know yet, that I was still very young. Even if I didn't feel very young. *Take these years to try out a lot of things so that you know what you like*, Mom liked to tell me. *You're smart. You're very young. You have plenty of time.*

Somehow I didn't think this was the right thing to say to the twelve-year-old girl who'd just declared she was going to be president not only someday, but at the earliest allowable age, since you can only run for president if you are thirty-five years old or older. "Maybe a fashion designer," I said. Julie had suggested that to me because I was always so interested in what people were wearing. She and Lexy used to ask me to dress them for all the bar and bat mitzvahs we went to. I loved going to the mall with them and wandering around and pairing them with clothes that not only looked beautiful with their coloring and body shapes, but that were also on sale. Julie was pale and blond, so she looked striking in dark, rich colors that contrasted with her skin. Lexy was very tall with brown hair even curlier than mine, so she could carry off a floor-length dress that made short people like me and Julie look like little kids playing dress-up in their moms' closets. "I'm really interested in clothes and things. And I think I'm good at it. I don't know. I'm still deciding."

"Interesting," Isabella said. "Is that a really high-paid job?"

I shrugged. "I have no idea."

"It must be," Isabella said. "Like, lots of fashion

designers are famous, right? Famous usually means lots of money."

A lot of money would be nice, but I didn't think I needed a humongous mansion and a fleet of cars to be happy. I shrugged again. "I don't know. Maybe."

She looked oddly disappointed for a moment, but I blinked, and then she perked up. "The bus is here. Let's go."

We climbed into the belching yellow monster. Isabella told the driver her address, and I followed her to the back, where she splayed out in one of the very back seats like it was hers by right. I was impressed. As a sixth grader, I'd never dared to venture all the way into the back where the eighth graders sat. I was a little worried they'd push me out the emergency door.

"If you really want to be a fashion designer, it's probably good to be friends with Elsa," she said. It took me a second to remember that Elsa was the golem. "Since her parents are a famous photographer and a model. Have you met them?"

I had to shuffle through all the stories Elsa'd been telling people, like a mental deck of cards. "Right, they are," I said. It was good I hadn't slipped and said something about skydiving. "I haven't met them, though. I think her mom is . . . sick." Better to stick with non-specifics. "So she isn't really having people over to her house."

"Yeah, that's what she said when I tried to hang out with her," Isabella said, looking disappointed for a second. But then she perked up again. That would be a useful quality in a president—being able to look happy on command. "I guess you don't really need her parents' help to get into fashion anyway, right? Not with your people."

My people? My mom did something with taxes, and my dad did something in an office having to do with machinery. Uncle Marvin and Aunt Jessie were teachers, and Zaide was a retired farmer/electrician. I didn't have any people in fashion, or know anyone even remotely connected to fashion, unless you counted faraway cousin Adelaide, who worked at a fancy boutique somewhere down south. Then again, I wasn't positive the fancy boutique actually sold clothes. It might have sold fancy soaps or fancy hand-knitted stuffed animals for fancy children.

But Isabella didn't have to know that. Not now that she'd (incorrectly) assumed I was much more interesting and well-connected than I actually was. "Right, my people," I said with a wave. I tried for an airy affect, too, one like I imagined the queen of England might use when talking about her butlers and drivers. "They're all so . . . fashionable."

"Cooool," she breathed. My insides clenched in worry that she'd ask more questions about these imaginary people, so I hurried to change the subject.

"So do you have any siblings?"

Isabella scrunched up her face. "Just one dumb brother," she said, but she didn't sound mean. Even when she pretended to gag. "Liam. He's almost nine, but I swear he acts like he's five. Don't worry, we can just pretend he isn't there."

"I always thought it would be kind of nice to have a brother," I said. When I was little, I'd beg Mom and Dad for one. That, or a sister. I wasn't picky. I wanted someone to dress up in costumes.

"Feel free to take mine," Isabella said. "Oh! This is our stop."

We got off in front of a house easily twice as big as my own. It looked like one of those houses I'd see while I was doing homework and my mom had HGTV on in the background: big and brick, with maroon shutters and a wide lawn. If it were a person, I decided, it would be a girl dressed up for a fancy occasion. Not a single strand of hair out of place, not a single stain on her fancy dress.

"My dad works from home, so he'll be here," she said as we climbed her front steps. "And Liam, of course. But like I said, feel free to pretend he doesn't exist."

I was already fantasizing about making Isabella's brother love me so much she'd have no choice but to have me come over all the time, but I said, "Okay."

The inside of Isabella's house was just as beautiful as the outside. The floors were a dark wood, and the walls were covered in patterned wallpaper in rich colors; professional photographs of Isabella, Liam, and their parents beamed at me from every surface between crystal vases and elegant glass animals. Isabella led me through the front hallway and beneath a grand staircase into a blindingly white kitchen. She went over to the fridge while I stared through the sliding glass door at a pool so clear and blue I wouldn't have been surprised to see a mermaid hoist herself onto the concrete and shake the water off her shimmering tail.

"What do you want?" Isabella asked me, and I was about to say *to live here* before I realized she was talking about a snack.

"Oh, um, I don't care," I said. "Whatever you're having."

"But there are things you can't eat, right?" she pressed. "Because you're Jewish?"

I shrugged. "I mean, my family doesn't strictly keep kosher," I said. "I don't eat pork, but that's pretty much it. And I'm not eating bread right now because it's still Passover, so maybe not a ham sandwich?"

I couldn't see her face, but the sigh she gave and the way her shoulders slumped a bit made it clear that she was disappointed again. But why? I would have thought she'd be happy not to have to worry about my dietary preferences. I said quickly, "I like yogurt?"

A minute later, we were sitting on the stools at the kitchen island, spooning yogurt with honey and granola into our mouths. "We have ice pops for after if you want," Isabella said around a mouthful of yogurt. "I'm not supposed to have them before dinner, but so what."

"So what," I agreed, feeling a little thrill at her daring.

Footsteps behind me. Before I could even turn around, Isabella rolled her eyes and groaned. "Go away, Liam."

"I'm hungry," Liam said. I was sure Isabella wouldn't like hearing this, but the two of them looked exactly alike, except that Isabella was older and had longer hair. They even wore identically annoyed expressions on their faces right now. "I'm allowed in the kitchen."

"Then get your food and go," Isabella said.

Of course, he didn't just get his food and go. If he were my brother, I had a feeling these antics would quickly get annoying, but to be honest, he was entertaining now. First, he walked incredibly slowly. Not just a stroll, but like he was losing a race against an exhausted snail. Every time Isabella huffed with frustration, he slowed down, so that after half a minute or so he was barely moving at all. A little smile played over his lips. He was very clearly enjoying this. Isabella looked as if she were about to burst into flames.

"So, what's your name?" he said, still not even halfway across the room.

"You don't have to answer that," hissed Isabella, but I didn't want to be rude. I could just imagine what my mom would say.

"Leah."

"That's a cool name. It sounds like my name, but it's not the same. I've never met another Leah, but there are, like, ten Liams in my grade." He actually stopped altogether now, his head tilting all the way to the side. "Isabella too.

It's a very *common* name." That didn't sound much like something an eight-year-old boy would say; I wondered if it was something Isabella had said to him. "It was on the top ten list for years. There are going to be a thousand Isabellas running for president in thirty-five years."

"In twenty-three years," Isabella replied. "In thirty-five years I'll have served my two terms, and I'll be out basking in the world's adoration."

"Not the *whole* world's, because you'll never have *mine*." Liam returned his attention to me. "What's your name mean?"

"I thought you were getting your food and leaving," Isabella said, but I was already answering. He was super cute. Like a baby bunny or something, it wouldn't stop jumping around, but you couldn't help but coo over it anyway. Maybe I *would* take him home.

I laughed a little. "I like my name, but it doesn't have the nicest meaning. My mom actually apologized to me when I looked it up. It's a Hebrew name meaning 'weary.' Like tired. I guess I *am* tired a lot from waking up early for school."

"Hebrew?"

"It's the language Jewish people pray in," I said. "They also speak it as an everyday language in Israel."

His eyes were way too wide for the boringness of the information I'd just given him. "Wait," he breathed.

You know that feeling you get when something is about to go horribly wrong? Like, the conscious part of your brain doesn't realize it yet, but the lizard part of it that's used to picking up on subtle movements and body language and maybe some psychic waves in the air knows, just *knows*, that something bad is about to happen? The one that's like a can of beans falling on your toe, except in your stomach?

That's what I was feeling right now.

"You're the Jewish friend," he said, and then he turned to Isabella. He lowered his voice in what might have been an attempt to keep me from hearing, but he was an eight-year-old boy. They only went so quiet. "Dad said you weren't supposed to invite her over."

Every part of my body froze. Even my heart. I swore I couldn't hear it thump, thump, thump anymore. Maybe I would die. Maybe that would be okay right now.

"Liam," Isabella hissed. "Shut up. I can do what I want."

Maybe if I stayed still enough, they would forget I was here. Maybe they'd think their parents had ordered a bizarrely Leah-shaped statue for their kitchen.

"I'm going to tell," he said, but he didn't move from his spot. Instead, he turned back to me. His eyes roved over me the way my mom looked over the fish she was going to buy at the supermarket's seafood counter. I almost expected him to step up and smell me. Would he throw me back if I didn't smell like the ocean? "Do your people really control the media and the government?"

"Liam!" Isabella snapped.

What was I supposed to say to that?

No, really, what was I supposed to say? Because I wasn't sure if I remembered any words. They'd all fled this beautiful house the way I suddenly wanted to.

Now Isabella's comment about how I wouldn't need any help getting into fashion made sense. Because she thought the Jewish octopuses would handpick me any job I wanted. And her comment about money, because that was another Jewish stereotype. And my head. She'd practically given me a head massage, and at that point I'd found that weird . . .

After a few seconds of silence, Isabella murmured, "I'm so sorry, I don't know where he got that from." And, somehow, that was enough to break me free.

"I'm going to the bathroom," I squeaked. I didn't know where the bathroom was, but in a house this big, there was probably one in every hallway. I fled down the closest hall, then stopped. What if I accidentally opened the door to the dad's office, and he saw my nose and immediately knew who—what—I was? Could I take that chance?

As it turned out, the door propped open right there was a bathroom. I sat on the lid of the toilet and called my mom.

"Leah? What's up?"

"Mom," I whispered into my phone. I bowed my head and curled into my shoulder. "I need you to come pick me up."

"What? I thought I wasn't coming to pick you up until five thirty." Her voice was so loud, even through the phone. Isabella and Liam could probably hear it in the kitchen. Their scary father could probably hear it from wherever his office was in this huge house. He would hear, and he would come and get me and—

"Please," I whispered. I cleared my throat, but it didn't stop my voice from breaking on the next part. "Please come pick me up."

A moment of silence on the other end. "Okay," she said. A rush of gratitude swelled within me. I loved her so much right now. "Okay, I'll leave now, but you'll have to come back to work with me." I would go to the doctor with her and voluntarily get shots if it meant getting out of here. "Be outside in twenty minutes."

A gush of relief filled me. I started the timer on my phone and counted a slow and agonizing seven minutes, which I figured was about as long as I could spend in there without Isabella starting rumors at school of an explosive diarrhea attack. I flushed and washed my hands thoroughly, scrubbing with hot water and soap, and then rubbed some of their probably expensive floral lotion into my stinging hands. By the time I left the bathroom and walked very slowly toward the kitchen, I estimated it had been at least eleven minutes. Maybe twelve.

Liam was gone, but Isabella was waiting for me. She leaped to her feet as soon as I crossed the threshold into the kitchen. "Leah!" she said. "I . . ." And she trailed off. We stared at each other. She looked expectant, like she was waiting for me to say something first. But I wasn't going to. What was I supposed to say to her? That it was okay she and her family didn't think of me as a person like her?

"Thank you for the yogurt," I said stiffly. No matter what else she'd said, I couldn't get over my mom's urges to be polite. I grabbed my backpack and slung it over my back. "My mom is coming. I should go wait outside."

"Wait," she said in a hurried whisper, blocking my way. "You didn't answer my stupid brother. Is any of that stuff true? Like, that you people control the media and the government and stuff? You could help me. I'll need to be class president in high school for my résumé. And then of course I'll need to get into the right college. Like, every president went to an Ivy League school. I'm aiming for Harvard or Yale, but Princeton would be okay, too."

I wanted to tell her no. I wanted to erupt at her about how stupid those beliefs were, how ridiculous, how absolutely insane. *If we control the world, why do people still hate us so much?* is what I wanted to say. *Why are there bomb threats all the time at my temple? Why aren't we rich? Why don't I have a house like yours?*

But my tongue was frozen. None of it would come out. It was like there was so much I wanted to say that my brain just short-circuited.

An ugly expression flickered over Isabella's face. "So you won't help me? That's not surprising. My dad says that Jews are selfish and greedy monsters."

Monsters? Then I remembered her running her fingers

through my hair and massaging my scalp and . . . She'd been looking for horns. That was another absurd Jewish myth. That we had horns. That we literally weren't people.

Tears prickled my eyes. I would shave my head right now if it would help show I was a person just like her.

My phone buzzed in my hand. I didn't have to glance down to know it was my mom. My whole body was itching to get out of here. I didn't have time for a perfect comeback. I just left. Who knew if the front door would lock behind me, but I didn't care. I wasn't ever coming back.

I was waiting at the passenger-side door of my mom's car before it even stopped. I didn't throw my backpack into the back like I usually did, just hopped in front and shoved it between my legs.

"What happened?" Mom asked. She looked over her shoulder and began to back out of the driveway. "You were so excited to hang out with this girl."

For some reason, now that I was actually getting away from Isabella and her house, the anger caught up with me. It swelled inside me, pushing my chest forward. Only, when I opened my mouth to yell, it was a sob that came out.

"Oh, Leah." A clicking noise from the turn signal, and my mom was pulling to the side of the road. "What happened?"

Before I could answer, she leaned over and hugged me. It was an awkward hug, since we were sideways and kind of forced to stay that way thanks to our seat belts, but it made me feel better nonetheless. Better enough that I told her exactly what had happened.

She was quiet while I spoke. When I finished, she sighed. "You know what Zaide says," she said. "The one thing that brings together the right and the left, the rich and the poor: making things up about the Jews." I'd definitely heard him say that before, only he used a way more vulgar expression for what everybody did.

It was a horrible thing to hear, but a laugh bubbled out of me anyway. The laugh tasted bitter in my mouth. I'd wanted to be Isabella's friend ever since I moved here. No, I hadn't wanted only to be her friend: I'd wanted to be just like her. And what had that gotten me? Nothing but a rotten feeling. "So what am I supposed to do?" I asked. "Her family didn't even know me. And yet they don't think of me like they would think of anybody else, just because of what I am."

She sighed again. "If I knew how to answer that, I would tell it to myself," she said. "We get bomb threats at temple all the time from people who don't know us or anything about us, but think they know everything."

My shoulders slumped.

"But I think that if people are going to hate you no matter what, you might as well be unapologetically yourself," Mom continued. "It's not like they're going to hate you *more* for it. You might even change some minds, though you shouldn't expect to and it's not your responsibility."

I sniffed. It wasn't what I wanted to hear. Then again, the only thing I wanted to hear right now was *Leah, wake up. It sounds like you're having a nightmare. Are you ready to go over to Isabella's and meet her family, who I hear love the Jews?* "What should I do, though? I'm going to have to face her in school on Monday."

My mom looked very old for a second. I didn't usually notice the wrinkles around her eyes or mouth, but right now they carved themselves deep into her face. "She's not your friend anymore. You can't be friends with someone who doesn't see you as a person."

"But then what . . ." I couldn't handle being thrown into the wilds of the cafeteria again. Not when I'd only just found a home.

"Thanks, Mom," I said anyway.

She looked at me a second longer. "It's going to be okay," she said.

I knew it, and she knew it. That she was lying.

CHAPTER SIXTEEN

I SPENT ALL WEEKEND WISHING for some freak meteor to come and strike all Mondays from the plane of existence or at least come and hit my house so that I wouldn't have to go to school. None of my wishing worked. I spent all of first and second period with my head down, frantically trying to find a solution for what I should do in the cafeteria. When lunch rolled around, my mind was as blank as ever.

Maybe I should eat in the bathroom. Wasn't that what bullied kids always did in books and movies? I stopped by the bathroom, my lunch bag grimly clutched in my hand, only to find a line and a group of girls from my class clustered giggling in front of the mirror.

I backtracked. There was a bathroom on the second floor that people never used because it was so far out of the way. I'd eat there. But when I went to go into the staircase, one of the monitors stopped me. "Where are you going?"

"Um, the bathroom," I said weakly. My palm was starting to sweat. My lunch bag was going to slip out of my hands and explode all over the floor, and everybody was going to laugh at me.

The monitor pointed behind me. "There's a bathroom over there. Use that one."

I dragged my feet as I walked away, yelling at myself in my head. *Stupid! You should have said your locker was up there, or you had to talk to a teacher.* But it was too late now. There was nowhere to go but the lunchroom.

I entered with my eyes trained straight ahead. I pretended I was one of those horses pulling carriages my parents and I saw in Central Park that time we went to New York City: wearing blinders that kept me from seeing anything to my sides. Was I imagining it, or did I hear whispering? Whispering that had to be directed at me? The back of my neck burned. My heart fluttered. It wasn't too late to turn around.

No, wait—it was. Because I could hear the golem

talking to me. I must be close to Isabella's table. Though I wouldn't know it, not with my blinders on. "Leah, where are you going?" she asked. Her voice was very loud. "Leah, I have a seat saved for you right here!"

My feet slowed. Would it really be so bad, to go and sit next to Isabella and pretend that nothing had happened?

My mom's voice echoed in my head. *You can't be friends with someone who doesn't see you as a person.* She was right. I couldn't sit there next to Isabella and pretend to laugh and talk, all the while knowing that she—and who knew who else at that table?—saw me as nothing more than a curiosity.

As I walked past, Elsa asked, "Isabella, did something happen at your house? Is she mad at you or something?"

"I have no idea." Isabella's voice sounded airy. "She's kind of weird anyway, isn't she? It's probably better if she . . ."

I couldn't hear her as I moved farther away. I was glad about that. I could only imagine what she was going to say next. *It's probably better if she sits somewhere else, where her giant nose won't put our whole table in shadow.*

The Three Ds still sat at their usual table in the back. It had been only a little over a week since I'd sat with them, but it seemed like it had been an entire year. They stared at me as I approached, not even pretending to glance around or anything.

The stares did not look friendly.

In fact, they looked more like glares.

"Hey," I said, trying to soothe the anger in the air with the warmth in my voice. It did not work. If anything, their faces hardened. "Um, is it okay if I sit here again?"

Silence. Something twisted in my chest. Maybe it was a symptom of a heart attack.

Dallas finally broke the ice. "What, you want to stoop to our level now that you got rejected or whatever by the popular kids?" she said, her voice like acid, and my chest twisted again because she was right. She was right, and it did not make me look good. Or feel good about it. "I'm so honored to know we're good enough for you now."

"That's not it at all," I said, though my voice came out weak. My stomach swam with something covered in tentacles. "You see the girl over there, the new girl? That's Elsa, my neighbor. She asked me to come sit with her, and—"

"You know we've been trying to be friends with you all year, right?" Deanna butted in. She was glaring at me for real now, her eyes hot under thick black brows. "I invited you over and everything. We kept talking to you and asking you questions, and you kept giving us these short little answers and playing on your phone, but you kept on sitting with us, so we figured you were just shy. But then we saw you over there"—she pointed emphatically, like I had no idea where she was talking about—"and you were chatting away with Isabella and her friends."

"Which means you just didn't like us." Daisy looked wounded rather than angry, her eyes huge and sad.

My heart was galloping. I couldn't seem to get enough air. They were wrong. Because they hadn't wanted to be my friends. I'd been sitting here for ages, and they'd been looking at my nose, and they hadn't invited me to their party, and . . . and . . .

"So you can go off and sit with Isabella and them again." Dallas set her juice box on the table hard. A little spurt of juice came up through the straw and splashed on the table, but she didn't go to wipe it away. "You can't sit with us."

"But I thought . . . I thought . . ." My voice came out as a squeak. This was wrong. This was all wrong. My head was spinning. How could I have gotten it so wrong?

I took a step back. I couldn't handle their eyes on me. I sucked in a breath, but it was like trying to squeeze a whole lungful of air through Dallas's juice box straw. It wasn't going in. I was going to die here, under all these judgmental eyes.

"Leah Nevins. Leah Nevins."

The sound of my name prickled over me like static. I looked around to find where it was coming from, and I realized that it did sound like static. It was coming from the loudspeaker, which was barely audible over the din in the cafeteria.

"Leah Nevins, please report to the front office."

Deanna scoffed. "Maybe they're giving you detention for being a sucky friend."

My eyes stung, but I had no retort for that. Except: *friend*? Why couldn't they have called me that before? I spun and walked away.

I'd never been so happy to be called down to the principal's office. My heart slowed, and I was able to suck in more air once I was safely in the quiet emptiness of the hallway. I walked as quickly as I could, my foot-steps loud on the scuffed tile floor. My relief was slowly trickling into worry. I might never have been so happy to be called to the principal's office . . . because I'd never *been* called to the principal's office. For all I knew, the office might actually have been a dungeon, with thumbscrews scattered about and chains hanging from the ceiling to stretch misbehaving students. Like me? I racked my brain for anything I could possibly have done to get myself in trouble. I'd yawned in class this morning and the teacher had given me a *look*, but I didn't think that was principal's-office worthy.

The confusion grew from a seed into a creeping vine when I entered the office to find my dad sitting in one of the principal's nubby orange chairs. The chairs were kid-size, meant for students waiting to see the principal, so his tall body looked strange in it, his knees crumpled up toward his chest. He stood as soon as he saw me, though.

"Leah," he said, and the seriousness in his tone made me stop short in my tracks. All my thoughts about Isabella and the Three Ds and the various lunch table catastrophes flew out of my mind. Something bad had happened. I immediately thought of my mom. Why else wouldn't she be here, if she wasn't flattened on the side of the road or—

"It's Zaide," my dad said, and I brought my hand up to my mouth. To prepare myself for what was coming? I didn't know. "We need to go right away."

CHAPTER SEVENTEEN

BEFORE TODAY, I'D BEEN TO a hospital twice. The first time was when my grandma on my dad's side was sick, but I barely remember that because I was like three years old. All I could remember was the shelf of get-well-soon bears in the gift shop, all smiling at me beneath their beady black eyes.

The second time was when I was eight years old, and I was trying to balance on the curb at a parking lot, and I sliced my palm open on the jagged edge of a license plate and had to get stitches. We sat in the emergency room for two hours while blood ran down my fingers and made a puddle on the floor. A little kid running around slipped in it and fell and hit his head.

It was a convenient place to do that. And even though he seemed perfectly fine aside from a little bruise, they rushed him back before me, which was unfair if you asked me. Which no one did.

This time was worse. Way worse. Dad spoke with the woman at the front desk and then zipped us upstairs in a shiny metal elevator that pushed us into a blindingly white hallway that smelled like Lysol and something else. Like death. Except I didn't know what death smelled like. It could actually have been meat loaf or something.

I floated down the hallway as if I were in a dream, tethered to this white world by only my dad's hand. We passed open doors and closed doors, some with name tags on them. I peeked through the open doors and cringed at everything I saw. A kid in what appeared to be a full-body cast, parts of it suspended from the ceiling. An old woman moaning in pain. Another old woman— not super old, though, like Mom old—lying still in bed, staring blankly at the TV overhead. The TV was off.

Zaide's room was at the end of the hall. We entered to find Mom already there, sitting beside Zaide's bed and holding his hand. His eyes were closed, his chest moving evenly up and down. His mouth gaped open, though, exposing his jumble of teeth. I hung back in the doorway. There were tubes and lines going in and out of him; a bag by the side of the bed was full of yellow liquid that had to be urine. A thick white cast covered half of one side of his body, starting at his waist and stretching down his leg.

Dad tugged me farther inside the room, but I resisted. My insides swirled with horror. This wasn't right. Zaide shouldn't be here. This shouldn't be Zaide. He didn't even *look* like Zaide.

He just looked like an old, old man.

"You'll get to sign his cast, Leah." My mom's voice creaked with exhaustion, like she hadn't slept in days. Even though she'd slept later than me this morning. "Isn't that nice?"

Are you losing your mind? is what I wanted to say. Instead, I said, "What happened?" Dad had told me a little bit on the ride over—that Zaide had broken his hip and that broken hips were very serious for old people, who had fragile bird bones—but he didn't know how it had happened. *I'm just as clueless as you, Leah*, he'd said, which was something he said sometimes when it was not true. I hoped I wouldn't feel clueless and lost at fifty or however old he was.

My mom's lip twitched, and I realized that she'd said

that about the cast because otherwise she really might lose it, having to think about all this. So I said, "You don't have to talk about it if you don't want to," but she was already talking. The lip twitch stopped, and she didn't burst into tears, so maybe it was good for her to get it out.

"I stopped by his house this morning as I was heading in to work. His car was there, but he wasn't inside, and I panicked." Her eyes got faraway, and I knew she was thinking about those Alzheimer's people she'd told me about. The ones who forgot where and who they were and wandered off and got hit by a car or fell off a cliff. "I was about ready to call nine-one-one when I heard him moaning from the side of the house."

I sucked in a quick breath. I could picture the scene: Zaide, crumpled on the ground, his skinny stick legs bent beneath him. Bald and pink like a baby bird fallen from the nest before it could fly.

"The TV wasn't working."

We all turned toward the bed. Mom made a sound somewhere between a gasp and a sob. Zaide's eyes were open but dreamy. Like he still wasn't all the way here because he was busy looking at something somewhere else.

"I had to fix the antenna," he said. It was even harder to understand him than usual because in addition to the thick Yiddish accent and no-teeth lisp, his voice was slurred with whatever pain medication they had him on. "The TV wasn't working. I had to fix it."

Mom squeezed his hand. "You should rest," she said, her voice trembling a bit. "Close your eyes."

"I had to fix it," he continued, as if she hadn't spoken at all. "The ghost couldn't stop me. None of her threats could keep me inside."

I froze, certain that my whole thing with the golem was about to come crashing down on me, and maybe I would deserve it because Zaide being here was at least partially my fault. But my parents only sighed. Both at once, like they'd rehearsed it out in the parking lot before my dad had come to get me. "Ghosts aren't real," my mom said patiently. "You should get some rest."

Ghosts might not have been real, but golems . . . if the golem was threatening him, I should know. Anger rushed hot through me. "Zaide, what ghost?"

"Leah," my dad began, like he was about to lecture me, but Zaide was evidently eager to talk about it.

"Maria's ghost," he said blearily. He closed his eyes and

didn't open them again, and my heart nearly stopped, but then they slowly opened. "She's back."

"Who's Maria?" I asked, but he continued on as if he hadn't heard me.

"She tells me to do things," he said. Mom and Dad exchanged a look over Zaide's bed. Oh no. This wasn't good.

I tried to stop him. "Zaide, maybe you should get some rest after—"

"If I don't want to do them, she tells me she'll tell everyone what happened, and my family will suffer." He blinked again, and when he opened his eyes, he looked bewildered. "I didn't mean it. I . . . Maria . . ." He launched into something in rapid Yiddish or Polish. His breathing came faster and faster, his eyes wilder and wilder. He bucked in his bed, pounded those frail bird arms against the railings. He shouted something I didn't understand. Then everything blurred before me, and I was being ushered out into the hallway while nurses rushed in.

This was my fault. All my fault.

I had to confront the golem. I had to make it stop.

But I couldn't leave Zaide right now. Both in a literal sense—my parents were here, and it wasn't like I could drive myself—and a metaphorical sense. He was hurting, and I couldn't bring myself to leave him alone in this awful place. So we sat there all day. When Zaide woke up, we told him jokes and reminisced about old family memories, and when he drifted off, we traded trips to the cafeteria for chips and ice cream bars. We stayed and we stayed and we stayed because that was what family did.

CHAPTER EIGHTEEN

WHEN UNCLE MARVIN SHOWED UP, he told us to go home. "Are Matty and Jed coming?" I asked, but he shook his head.

"They're going to come tomorrow. Guys, go home. I'll take things from here."

Our car ride home was silent, aside from the DJ laughing on the radio. "Can you—" I began, but my dad didn't wait for me to finish before pressing the off button and plunging the car into blissful silence. I looked out the window and imagined rain streaking down the glass like teardrops. In reality it was a clear night, the moon high and bright above because Mother Nature had no decency.

I was grateful for the silence. My hands balled into fists at my sides. I was going to find the golem. She'd betrayed me. She'd been mean, and she'd threatened Zaide, and she hadn't listened to me, which basically meant that Zaide's breaking his hip was her fault. Her. Fault. My nails bit into my palms.

And she'd been doing this by pretending to be someone from Zaide's past. Someone it hurt him to think about. Why? Zaide was so gentle and kind. What could this person have done to him? I'd ask the golem a few questions, and then I would return her to the dust.

Mom and Dad went right up to bed at home, claiming to be wiped out. If you asked me, Mom just wanted to cry. Which she could have done in front of me, because I kind of wanted to cry, too. But no one ever asked me.

So be it. I had to find the golem.

I strode quickly down the sidewalk, the bright light from the streetlights overhead bathing me in warmth. I waved at the dog walkers, then walked up Zaide's driveway. The door didn't open.

Right. He wasn't home, so it would be locked. I dug my keys out of my pocket. It took me a few tries to wrestle the old, heavy door open with the key. I wasn't sure I'd ever actually used it before.

Zaide's house felt dark and small without him in it. Though he hadn't done any cooking in it today, it still smelled of chicken broth and steamed whitefish. I breathed the smell in deep, letting it flow through me and comfort me. Zaide would be back. He just had to heal. Jed had broken his arm once after jumping on the bed, and all he had to do was wear a cast for a while. That was the arm he pitched with today. You'd never even know it had been broken.

It's different for really old people, that traitorous part of my mind whispered, but I shut it down. I didn't need to listen to it right now.

"Elsa?" I called. I turned, taking in every inch of the house I could see from here. The gleaming stretch of the table. Zaide's newly neat desk with the rolly chair. The red velvet couch. The glimpses of bedrooms revealed by their open doors.

No golem in sight. No tendrils of brown hair reaching out from under the couch or table or bed. "Elsa?" I called, taking a step toward the kitchen. She didn't seem to be in there, either. "Elsa?"

If she wasn't here, then where could she be? I turned in another circle, then collapsed into Zaide's rolly chair.

Hopefully she wasn't at the hospital. Could she be at Isabella's house or something?

I pushed off, and the chair whirled me in a circle, whirling my thoughts around with it. The chair slowed to a stop, but I pushed off again, sending me around and around so fast that the base of the chair rattled like an earthquake was coming. "Woo!" I cried. I couldn't believe Zaide had never let us spin in the chair before. That he kept something so much fun from us.

The room was a blur. Blurry table. Blurry desk. Blurry table. Blurry desk. Blurry girl—wait. I slammed my feet on the floor, bringing the chair to a lurching stop. For a moment the world around me kept on spinning, but as soon as it stopped, I jumped to my feet. "There you are," I said to the golem, who was standing in front of the table, her arms folded. Her face was in shadow.

"Here I am," she agreed. The light reached her body, so I could see she was wearing a new outfit, one that looked like she could've ripped it right out of a magazine page: a short denim skirt with a flap in the front over distressed leggings with a tucked-in baggy white shirt that said FREE SPIRIT. The shoes on her feet were snakeskin ballet slippers with silver buckles on top. Where had she even gotten all of these? Had she stolen them? I opened my mouth to ask her, but other stuff came out instead because, *right*, I had way more important things to worry about at this moment.

"Zaide is in the hospital, and it's your fault," I said. I paused to give those words their proper weight. It wouldn't be out of line, I thought, if she collapsed to her knees to beg my forgiveness. Maybe even kissed my sharp purple sneakers.

Instead, she shrugged. "It wasn't like I pushed him off the ladder."

"You were supposed to keep him safe," I accused. "That means keeping him off the ladder in the first place."

She shrugged again. "There's only so much I can do."

"Yeah." I scoffed. "Like threaten him." I paused again and waited to see what she would say to that. Whether she'd deny it, or whether she'd be proud of her villainy.

"Maybe you should ask him about it," she said.

"Or you could just tell me whatever you think you know."

"I don't actually know anything for sure," she said airily. "Not the full story. All I know is that he's afraid of this Maria person I look like and that he panics when I threaten to tell everybody what he did to me."

My shoulders relaxed. I hadn't even realized, but they'd gotten all bunched up around my ears. "So you don't know anything."

She just raised her other eyebrow. Basically saying, *Yes, I do. More than you, Leah.*

I wondered if she remembered any of her past lives. She was made of the same dirt, after all.

That didn't matter, though. "Look," I said, and paused because she'd stepped forward, bathing herself in light. Including her face. I sucked in a breath.

The side of her face was crumbling. From her ear down to her chin, an inch- or two-wide stretch down the left side had gone brown and crumbly as dirt. The destruction was tugging at the corner of her left eye, pulling it down. The effect was that she seemed to be suffering from some horrible skin disease and a stroke at once.

She saw me staring. Her lips turned down into a pout. "I'm getting ugly now," she said. "I can't be popular and loved if I'm so ugly. You need to fix me."

"Sure," I agreed. I took a step toward her. "I just need to resculpt your face a bit, and you'll be good as new."

She smiled. As she spoke, her *shem*-stamped tongue came into sight. "Maybe you can even make me more beautiful than before. I'll be more popular than Isabella Lynch."

"Sure," I agreed again. I tried to make my voice sound as soothing as a lullaby. Maybe I could lull her into falling asleep. That would make this so much easier. "Whatever you want."

She continued speaking as she moved closer. Her tongue flashed into view with every word. "Maybe some ombre at the bottom of my hair. Or highlights. Or streaks of green. I think that might look really cool. No—blue!"

I kept nodding and smiling. If I reached out now, I could touch her shoulder. Another step. If I reached out now, I could brush her chin. Another step. If I reached out now, I could—

"And my forehead is a little too big, don't you think? I want a smaller forehead this time, and even higher cheekbones, since my mom is supposed to be a model, and—"

My hand darted out toward her mouth. I could feel the strange dry chill of her breath on my fingertips and—

Her own hand gripped my wrist with inhuman strength. It clamped on like an iron manacle. I struggled, trying to free it, but even if I managed to escape her iron grip, her mouth was closed now, her head pulled back.

"What do you think you're doing?" Her voice was deadly quiet and just a little bit muffled, since she was keeping her mouth closed as much as she could.

There was literally nothing I could say that would make me sound good. So I stared at her mutely, biting my own tongue to keep from shrieking in pain. Her grip was *hard*. My last year's gym teacher, who was intense about handshakes and how we'd need a firm handshake to make it in high school and the real world, would have been beyond impressed.

"You were trying to rip out my tongue." She answered her own question. "Are you sick of me, Leah? You don't need me anymore, so you thought you'd kill me?"

It's not killing if you're not real is what I wanted to say. But my voice seemed to have shriveled up. Because for the first time, I really understood that she and I were alone in Zaide's house. In Zaide's house with the walls made of brick three feet thick.

Nobody was going to hear me if I screamed.

She leaned in. When she spoke, I could smell the earthiness of her breath. "Maybe I should rip out *your* tongue and see how *you* like it."

My breath caught. I wanted to say something in response, but that would involve opening my mouth.

And I didn't want to take the chance of opening my mouth.

She smirked. "I thought so." She pushed me away, letting go of my arm. Again, her strength was inhuman. I went flying backward and would have fallen if the rolly chair hadn't caught me and skidded.

Now that she was beyond reaching distance, I could speak. "I didn't mean to hurt you," I said, trying for that calming tone of voice again. *My mom trying to soothe me after a nightmare.* "I was just trying to make you beautiful again, like I—"

She snorted, stopping me short. "Like there's even a chance I'm going to believe that," she said scornfully. "You know, Leah, I might be getting a little ugly, but at least I'm not ugly like *you.*"

She took a step closer, casting her eyes over me from top to bottom. I could barely breathe. "Look at that nose of yours. You freak. You can't even see the rest of your face behind it."

I was not going to cry. Not when I knew she was specifically trying to hurt me. So I was not going to let her make me cry. I swallowed hard.

Definitely not.

"No wonder you can't make any friends. Who would

want to be friends with a freak like you?" She sneered. She took another step closer. "And no wonder Isabella hates you. You're hideous. You can put whatever clothes you want on your body—it won't change that face."

Definitely.

Not.

I balled my fists, like that might intimidate her and stop her from coming at me. I might also be balling them up at myself. Here I was, trapped in a house with a monster, and I was worrying about my nose. I shook my head.

I just wanted to make her stop voicing all my worst fears into the real world outside my head. "You can't kill me," I said. "They'll find you. They won't let you go."

She scoffed again. "I know I can't kill you. Not if I want to keep my life and make it even better. But I don't need to hurt *you* to get you to do what I want, Leah. That's what I learned at the seder. I just didn't do a good enough job." She smiled toothily. I was left with the impression that she had too many teeth to fit in her mouth. "Just wait and see."

She took a step back. I couldn't let her go. I lunged toward her, but a shrill ring tore into the air. An alarm? Was something—

The Christmas lights began flashing overhead, splashing her face and my face and the world around us with bright spots of red and blue and green. The phone. The phone was ringing.

I focused back on the golem. But there was no golem to focus on. She was gone.

I swallowed hard again, and it felt like I had swallowed a stone. It landed with a thunk in the pit of my stomach. This was not good. No, this was decidedly Not Good.

I don't need to hurt you *to get you to do what I want, Leah.* Her words ran through my head like a neon marquee sign. What had she meant? She didn't plan to hurt me, which was good.

But she'd emphasized that first *you*. Which made it sound like she wasn't going to hurt me . . . but that she might hurt other people. And out of all the people I knew, there was someone frail and old and fragile. If she hurt him, it would hurt me a whole lot.

I had to get to Zaide right away.

CHAPTER NINETEEN

MY PARENTS DID NOT UNDERSTAND my urgency.
At this point I would have been willing to tell them the
whole story with the golem if I'd thought they'd believe
me and not decide I was making things up and that I had
to go to bed right now. Since that was not the case, I had
to settle for something else.

"I just have a really bad feeling that something terrible
is going to happen to Zaide if we're not there," I said.
"Like right now. We need to go to him right now."

Mom sighed. She was sitting on the edge of their bed
wearing her sick pajamas, aka the ones she wore when
she had to stay home from work sick. They were big and
baggy and the ugliest things I'd ever seen, with brown

and red and green plaid, but they'd been washed so many times they were as soft as the insides of my forearms. "We need to get some sleep," she said. "I know this is a scary time. We'll feel a little better in the morning."

I bristled all along my back. "First of all, I'm not a baby," I said. "And please? Please, please, please. I'll feel so much better if we could just pop in on him and make sure he's safe and maybe hire an armed guard to keep him that way?"

"Leah." Dad was leaning against the doorway to the bathroom. He'd skipped shaving, I guess, so the bottom half of his face was covered in a dark brown shadow of stubble. "Nobody is going to hurt Zaide in the hospital. I promise you that, okay?"

I swallowed down my frustration. "You don't know that."

"Leah." This was Mom, reaching for her nightstand. "Uncle Marvin is still with Zaide right now, I think. Why don't we give him a call? We can make sure Zaide is okay?"

Great. So the golem would hurt Zaide *and* Uncle Marvin. "Fine," I said. It was better than nothing, I supposed.

According to Uncle Marvin, everything at the

hospital was fine. There were even security guards on every floor to keep anyone suspicious out. Not that they would stop the golem, who could golem magic herself wherever she wanted. "I'm going to spend the night," he told me. "So anyone coming after Zaide will have to go through me!"

I tried to console myself with that. Even if the golem was extra strong, she was still my size. She'd have a lot harder time fighting her way through Uncle Marvin without making a loud commotion than if she just attacked poor Zaide asleep in his bed.

"And I'm going in tomorrow morning," Mom said. "Dad will pick you up from school and take you, too. So we'll see him tomorrow, all right?"

My shoulders sagged. My whole body sagged, actually. I'd never felt so helpless. "Okay."

Thus passed a sleepless night. I was just about to drift off when my eyes popped open. It wasn't like the golem had specifically said she was going to hurt Zaide, just people who weren't me. What if she meant my parents? I couldn't exactly keep watch over my parents all night, so instead, I lay in my bed and listened hard for any sounds out of the ordinary. At some point I must have fallen asleep, because the ordinary sounds included the usual overhead flight of a flock of owls with wind chimes for wings. But I woke up in the morning to find my whole, healthy parents in the kitchen drinking coffee, so it all turned out okay.

At school, I shrank into the background as much as I could, and I'd wised up to the monitor in the stairwell during lunch, who let me up to the second floor when I told her I was meeting a teacher upstairs. Lunch in the bathroom had never been so depressing. (Or smelly.)

After the last bell, my dad met me outside. "How was school?"

"Fine," I said. Was it actually possible to answer that question any other way? It wasn't like I was going to be like, *Actually, it was terrible. I ate lunch in a bathroom today. How was work? I bet you didn't eat lunch in a bathroom.*

We spent most of the trip in silence. I leaped out of the car as soon as we parked, but I didn't get very far, since I had to wait for Dad to leave the parking garage with me. I vibrated with impatience the whole trip up to Zaide's floor. I had to see him to know he was okay. I had to . . . I held my breath as we walked down the hallway. Dad wasn't walking fast enough, so I forged ahead, not fast enough to get yelled at for running, but definitely faster. Just a few more doors—there was the sad kid in the cast, there was the woman staring at the blank TV, and there...

There was Zaide. Lying down in his bed, his eyes open, talking to Mom. I heaved a great sigh of relief. He was okay. Well, as okay as he could be with a broken hip. But at least the golem hadn't made things worse.

Yet.

I had to warn him. Given that Elsa had been made from the same clay as his golem, and he was the one who'd told me about it in the first place, he was probably the only adult who would believe me. That meant I had to get Mom and Dad out of the room.

I could try to trick them into getting me something from the cafeteria or somehow find a way to lock them in the bathroom, but the thought of all that tired me out. To be quite honest, I was getting sick of lying. "Mom, Dad," I said. "Can I have a minute alone with Zaide? Or ten minutes, actually. A minute is too short."

They exchanged a look. To be quite honest again, I was getting sick of people exchanging looks with each other over my head, too. "Please," I said. "I just want to talk to him."

Mom stood up from where she sat at his side and crouched down beside me so that her mouth was at my ear level. "You know, Leah, he's not entirely lucid right now," she whispered. "You might want to wait until later."

Except that this couldn't wait. Not another minute. "I just want to talk to him," I repeated. Mom and Dad gave each other another look, and then Mom stood up and sighed.

"Honey, let's head down to the cafeteria for ten minutes. I saw a salad earlier that didn't look terrible. Leah, will you be okay for ten minutes?"

That was literally what I had just asked for, but I knew if I said that, Mom would get mad at me for giving her attitude. "Yes," I said impatiently.

"If . . . You know, if there's any trouble, the nurses' station is right out there. Pressing this button will call them."

"Okay."

It took them longer than it should have to leave; they kept looking over their shoulders at me like I was going to explode or something. I *was* going to explode if they didn't get out of here, but from annoyance.

Finally, they were gone. I listened to their footsteps

go all the way down the hall, and then I took my mom's chair beside Zaide. I gently took his hand and held it between both of mine. It was cold. I held it tighter to warm it up, wishing I had four hands so I could warm his other one, too. Except that there were all the tubes and stuff coming in and out of that one. My stomach did a flip-flop.

I turned my attention to his face. He was squinting blearily at me. "Zaide, it's me," I said. "Leah. Your great-granddaughter." And since Matty and none of the far-away cousins were here, I went on with, "Your *favorite* great-granddaughter."

He stared at me a moment longer, his eyebrows knitted together. But then his face relaxed, and his head gave a little bounce. A nod from a lying-down position. "Rosie," he said. "Rosie, of course I know you."

Rosie? Who was Rosie?

I would just have to roll with it. I had only ten minutes. Less than ten minutes now. I hoped he would remember what I had to tell him. "Look, Zaide," I said. "This is important, so try to remember. Do you remember when you told me about the golem? The whole story about sixteenth-century Prague or whatever, and how you found it and made your own?"

He just squinted at me again and frowned. I guessed I had to take that as a yes. "So, I actually found the remains of your golem in the garage," I said. "And it was a stupid, stupid thing to do, but I made my own. It was Elsa. You met Elsa. You thought her name was Maria."

Zaide's face collapsed in on itself. That was the only way to describe his expression. I shouldn't have mentioned Maria.

But now it was too late. "The golem," he said. There was a sob thick in his voice, one long and extended, like it had no beginning or end. "I made the golem. After all that happened with Maria, the golem attacked us. That's the end of every golem story, you know. They turn on their creator."

My blood seemed to freeze. "Why didn't you tell me that before?"

"The golem of Prague went on a murderous rampage in the Jewish section of the city when the rabbi lost his control." Zaide's voice was a mourner's dirge, the way we say the Kaddish to remember those who have died. "Maria was my friend, though she was not Jewish. This was the 1930s, when the Holocaust was unfolding and such friendships were rare . . . and discouraged. Maria's family was kind, but her neighbors supported the efforts to kill all of us. Do you know how many Jews died in the Holocaust, Rosie? Our population a hundred years ago was higher than our population now."

His voice shuddered. "I had feelings for her. One night, Maria and I kissed. Her neighbor saw. Maria spoke up in my defense, but her neighbor shouted for his friends to come and kill me for the crime of defiling a non-Jewish girl with my Jewish lips. The golem was supposed to save us."

"But it didn't," I said, dreading what was sure to come next.

"It didn't," Zaide said. "I told the golem to defend us, but it turned on us instead. It killed . . ." Now his breathing shuddered, too. "The golem looks for loopholes in your rules, wherever it can find them." I'd certainly noticed that. "I told it to protect us from the non-Jews. And Maria was a non-Jew. It did not matter, that we did not need protecting from her. It killed her anyway." He closed his eyes for a moment, as if sharing the news still hurt, however many years ago it had happened. "The non-Jews thought it was us. And in a way, it was. It was my fault. The rest of us had to run, or they would have killed us all." Zaide paused for a moment, letting the gravity of his words sink in. "And it was lucky we did, or we would all have been killed in the Holocaust."

I had no idea what to say. I mean, I was actually at a loss for words. There wasn't anything I could say to make that hurt better.

"You should not have created a golem, Rosie," Zaide said, his voice grave now.

Tears pricked my eyes. "I'm sorry. I'm so sorry. I know I shouldn't have. I just wanted to help. I wanted to make it so you didn't have to leave, so that Mom and Dad wouldn't send you away." I sniffled. "Though, it would have helped if you'd told me about the murderous-rampage thing and how they always turn on their creator. Maybe you should have mentioned that? Anyway. Now I have to stop her before she can do something bad, like yours did. She's threatening me because she wants to be beautiful and popular, no matter what. Remember at Passover? I'm afraid she's going to hurt you, Zaide."

"You don't need to worry about me." He raised the arm I was holding and flexed it. Despite the seriousness and the sadness hanging over the room right now, I couldn't help but laugh. "I pull plows with this arm. If someone came after me, I'd jump out of this bed and wrestle them to the ground."

I wondered who Zaide was in his head. He must be thinking he was still young and strong, pulling plows. Maybe in his brain it was sixty years ago. Sixty years ago, he would have been thirty-three, running his chicken farm, raising his three young kids.

Rosie. That was it. My grandmother Roslyn, the one I was named after. Zaide's daughter. My Zaide thought I was her.

I laid my cheek down on the bed beside Zaide's own head. This close I could see the marks of age on his face: the brown sunspots, the pockmarks from bug-bite scars. His nose arching high and proud from his face. I sighed. "What am I supposed to do?"

He couldn't turn all the way over to his side, not with the cast and all the tubes, but he did turn his head so that he was looking directly into my eyes. A little bit down at me, actually, because his head was propped up on a pillow. It didn't feel like he was looking down *on* me, though. Zaide would never look down on me, no matter how short I was. Which was very.

He said, "You have to fix it, Rosie. You started it, and you have to end it."

I sniffled. My eyes were welling up. I hoped they wouldn't well over and make spots on Zaide's sheets.

"But that's how this whole thing started. I was trying to fix everything, and I just made it all more of a mess."

"That's life."

His pronouncement was so frank and so nonchalant that I burst into laughter. And tears. There were definitely going to be water spots on Zaide's sheets. It took a second for my laughter to subside, and then he went on.

"That's what life is, Rosie. There are some things you can control and some things you can't. Some things you can fix, and that you should fix, and some things that you can't. Life is all about figuring those things out for what they are, and being patient and accepting of the things outside of your control." He sighed. "I'm still learning that."

I sighed in response, fluttering the corners of his pillowcase. I wished I could climb into the bed and hug him, but I was afraid of jostling those tubes or hurting him in his cast. "But how do I know what I can fix and what I can't?"

"You don't." Again, his frankness brought on a slightly hysterical bout of giggles. "You don't always know, Rosie. Sometimes you do. Sometimes you have to try and fail. Sometimes you have to try and succeed. And sometimes there's a little voice inside you trying to speak the truth, and you have to listen to that voice."

I didn't know what voice he was talking about.

Yes, you do, insisted the voice.

I went to shut it out again, then stopped. He was right. I'd had this voice trying to talk to me this whole time, this voice from my conscience, and I just didn't want to hear it. I'd thought of it as a traitor.

Zaide can't be on his own anymore, Leah. You know it. You just don't want to know it.

I took a deep breath. "How do I . . .? If there's something I know I can't change, but it's something awful, how am I supposed to try to accept it?" Accept that my Saturday afternoons with Zaide and Jed and Matty were over. That Jed and Matty would never be as close to me as they were right now. That Lexy and Julie were making new friends and having a life without me that I couldn't be a part of. That Zaide would never be the same again, and that eventually he would die. And eventually my parents would die. I knew it was—hopefully—a long time off, but I still couldn't help the cold feeling in my chest.

"It's something you need to learn for yourself. It's

different every time." He was silent for a moment. "It's still something I'm trying to learn after all these years."

After Maria? After his family had been driven out of their home and people tried to kill them for no other reason than that they were Jews? He couldn't control that. He couldn't control any of that. He just . . . *we* just had to live with it. I guess there was no other option. We do what we can to change what we can, and otherwise we just have to deal with it.

"Thank you, Zaide," I said. I closed my eyes and nestled deep into the sheets.

"I love you, Rosie."

I opened my eyes in surprise as a cold, frail finger trailed down the bridge of my nose. I had to fight the urge to yank my face away—I didn't want to jar any of the tubes or hit his cast. But just drawing attention to my stupid nose had ruined all the peace I was feeling. I jerked away.

"What's wrong?"

I said nothing. I didn't even want to dignify this . . . this stupid appendage with a response.

"Is it your nose?" he said gravely.

How did he know? I nodded into the sheets.

He sighed. "You know, your mother has the same insecurities," he said. "You have her nose."

Bubbe Ruth? And Grandma Roslyn? I'd seen pictures of both—they hung in our house—but from when they were way older than I was. Sure, their noses weren't small, but they weren't as big as mine, as the nose I got stuck with from Zaide. Though they weren't really that different looking, I guess. Their noses were high and regal and proud, and they fit their faces. It made them look high and regal and proud, too. Like the coins of one of those old Roman emperors. Or empresses.

"Your mother was the most beautiful woman I had ever seen," Zaide told me. Then stopped and considered. "Is. She still is. But when I saw her, Rosie? She was my neighbor when we came to the States. I saw her in the hallway of our building, and I stopped short in my tracks."

Beautiful? Not with *this* nose. He must have been more senile than I thought.

"She hated her nose. What she didn't realize was that it suited her." He scratched his chin. It sounded like paper tearing. "She would not have been suited with an ordinary nose. That nose was hers, the nose that was passed down from noble farmers dreaming of Jerusalem and their ancestors, the priests in the great temple. Strong and confident, and she always knew what she wanted. She was a big person, and she needed a big nose."

He poked my nose at the tip. "And you, Rosie? You'll grow into it."

That was something my parents sometimes said. *You'll grow into it.* Meaning that, I guess, my face would get bigger and my nose wouldn't and somehow they would balance each other out.

But it didn't sound like that's what Zaide was saying. Somehow I felt like he was saying I needed to grow on the inside to be worthy of this nose. To be worthy of the nose of ancient priests and Nazi fighters and Bubbe Ruth and Grandma Roslyn. That someday I would be strong and confident and big enough that I'd need a nose like this to lead my way.

I didn't feel like it.

CHAPTER TWENTY

I DIDN'T SAY ANYTHING TO Zaide about what he'd told me about my nose. Which was just as well because he quickly began to snore. I sat up and wiped my cheeks with the back of my hand. I didn't want my parents seeing me cry and asking me why. So annoying. I went into the bathroom to splash my face with water and hopefully bring the redness down. By the time I came out, my parents were back, coffees in hand. My mom was staring down at her phone, her lips pursed into a frown.

"Everything okay?" I asked so that she couldn't ask it of me first.

She shook her head absently. "It's just strange. Uncle

Marvin and Aunt Jessie and Jed and Matilda should have been here ages ago. And they're not texting me back."

I immediately thought, *Car accident, earthquake, lightning strike, they're all dead.* I swallowed that dread—they were probably not all dead—probably—and said, "That's weird. Maybe there's traffic and their phones are dead. Or not getting a signal."

"Maybe," my mom replied. She began punching buttons on the screen. "I'll try Zaide's house. They were supposed to stop by and pick up some of his clothes and things."

Oh.

Oh no.

I don't need to hurt you *to get you to do what I want, Leah.*

When I'd created the golem, I'd been annoyed at Matty and Jed for being in denial. For not helping me. And if the golem had absorbed my feelings on everything else . . .

She hadn't come after Zaide. Or my parents.

My mom sighed and pulled the phone away from her ear. "Not answering. Maybe they're close? Let's give it ten minutes. Zaide's house isn't far."

We gave it ten minutes that felt more like ten

thousand minutes. I chewed on the inside of my cheek the whole time to keep from screaming. Something was wrong. Not just wrong. Very wrong. I felt it in my bones. And the longer we waited, the worse it could be.

"I left my thing at Zaide's house." The words jumped out of me before I could fully process them in my head.

"What was that?" Dad asked.

"My very important . . . homework. Book I have to read," I invented. "I left it at Zaide's last time I was there. And it's due tomorrow. Oh no!"

I was not going to win an Oscar anytime soon, but my fake horrified face was enough to get my mom looking worried. She turned to my dad. "Do you think you could . . ."

"Say no more." Dad motioned to me.

I tagged after him as he strode through the hallway, through the reception area, through the parking garage, into the car. "Hey," I said, once we were on the road. "Do you believe in magic?"

"Magic?" He scratched the back of his head. "I don't know—that's a pretty broad category. Do I think there are things that happen that we can't explain? Sure. Do I believe in wands and spells and *abracadabra*? Not so much." He was silent for a beat, maybe waiting for me to explain why I'd asked him that, then gave in. "Why do you ask?"

Because the golem made me wonder what else was out there. If golems were real, and it was possible to create an animated being with some dirt and a scrap of perhaps magic paper, what else *was* out there? What else was it possible to do with my own two hands? "I don't know," I said. "Like you said, there are things out there that happen that we can't explain."

"Like dark matter. And dark energy."

I vaguely knew what those were—parts of space that existed but that we couldn't see, that we didn't know what they were. "Right." Was the golem animated by dark energy? Was Hashem—God—somewhere in that dark matter?

We pulled up in front of Zaide's house. Dad frowned. My heart skipped a beat, lurching into my throat.

Uncle Marvin and Aunt Jessie's car was there, parked in the driveway.

"That's weird," Dad said. "That they wouldn't answer the phone if they were here."

Thump-thump. Thump-thump. Each heartbeat pushed thick black dread through my veins, a creeping sense of doom. "You wait in the car while I help them pack up," I said, already hopping out.

"Don't forget your book!" my dad called after me.

It took me a moment to realize what he was talking about and another moment for it to stop mattering altogether because I heard Matty and Jed screaming from the garage.

Forgetting that I was supposed to be looking for my book, I raced inside. It was dark in there, and for a moment, I couldn't see, and then my vision cleared, and there were the various farming machines and old furniture and pieces of Zaide's life all cluttered together, seething with shadows.

And the screaming. "Help!" Matty shouted. She'd clearly seen me; her eyes were widening, and not just with fear. "Help! Call nine-one-one!"

She and Jed were backed into a corner of the garage, caged in by a jungle of menacing farm equipment with blades and rusty claws. It was dark, so I couldn't see them that well, but they stood back to back, each of them entirely straight. It looked like they didn't have enough room to move without slicing an arm or a neck on one of those scary machines.

"Matty! Jed!" I started moving toward them, then stopped. The hairs were rising on the back of my neck. Because obviously this was golem work. These machines hadn't moved themselves into a makeshift prison.

"Welcome, Leah. I hoped you might come for the party."

I whirled to find the golem stepping out from behind a bookshelf. She stood a moment in its shadow, as if purposefully prolonging the suspense, before stepping out. I gasped.

The dirt part of her face from before? It had widened. It now took up a full half of her face: Her left eye was nothing more than a glint of black gravel, and her skin was packed dirt sculpted into the vague shape of a human head. She took another step forward, and grains of dirt sloughed off and fell to the floor with the sound of pattering rain.

Her mouth opened in a smile. My stomach lurched. One side of her mouth was surrounded by normal lips. The other side? There was a worm curled into the crumbling dirt of her skin, its two ends lashing against her face where her lips had once been.

"Elsa," I said, and my stomach lurched again, just from

calling a creature like that by a human name. "You have to let them go."

She waved her left hand in the air, and one of the blades hanging off the machines lurched, swinging close to Matty. Matty screamed, pressing back against Jed, which made him stumble closer to the machines on his side. Elsa was using her golem magic to terrorize my cousins. But when I looked closer, I saw what it had cost her. Part of her hand had crumbled off and pattered to the floor.

"I waited for you," the golem continued. "I wanted you to see what I've done. It wouldn't be any fun if you weren't here. This is what you want, isn't it?"

What I want? This was nowhere near what I wanted! The golem was supposed to be good and helpful and true. She was supposed to take care of Zaide so he wouldn't hurt himself. She was supposed to help me keep my family together, make things easier. Not let Zaide break his hip falling from a ladder, not threaten to impale my cousins with rusty farm equipment.

But then I remembered a sign I'd seen one time inside a fancy sandwich shop that had maybe the best turkey sandwich I've ever had in my life. It said MADE WITH

LOVE. I swallowed hard. I hadn't made the golem with love. I remembered biting my tongue with frustration as I'd mashed up her clay. I'd been resentful of everyone when I'd made her—of my parents for not listening, of Matty and Jed for their denial. And she'd absorbed that, the same way she'd absorbed my desire for popularity and impressive family stories, my desire to understand people.

"This is *not* what I want," I said, struggling to keep my voice under control and not let it turn into a shrill screech. "I want you to let them go, whole and healthy, so that they can go home with their family."

Uncle Marvin and Aunt Jessie weren't in here with Jed and Matty. What had Elsa done to them?

I pushed them to the back of my mind. First, we had to get rid of the immediate danger in here with us. "Please, Elsa," I said. "If you let them go, I can help you."

I stepped closer to her. "I can fix your face. Make you look pretty again. Isn't that what you want?" Another step. She watched me as if hypnotized. If I could just get close enough to rip out her *shem*-stamped tongue, I could end all this right now. "Let me fix you, and then we can both be beautiful and popular again."

She didn't have to know that Zaide's words were coming back to me, whispering silently in my ear. I couldn't fix everything. There were some things you just couldn't control. I'd created the golem to take care of Zaide, but it was impossible. Taking care of Zaide wasn't up to me. Some things could be up to only Hashem. Or whatever was out there.

I had almost reached the golem. Only a few more steps, and—

The golem's worm-lips twitched into a sneer. I stopped short, my heart racing. "Do you think you can fool me again? I won't let you trick me. You have to help me, whether you want to or not!" The blades around Matty and Jed clanged as if in agreement, drawing screams from my cousins.

I needed more time. More time to come up with a plan. There had to be something else I could say to fix this. To get more time, I had to get away from Elsa. She wouldn't hurt my cousins if I wasn't here to see it. She'd want to make sure hurting them hurt me.

So I plunged into the garage.

Shadows sprang up around me, menacing and awful. Every single one looked like the golem leering at me, about to pounce. I pushed my way through a rack of musty coats. Past a shelf of old magazines. Beneath a chandelier propped on the edge of a high shelf.

I jumped back just in time for the shelf to fall and the chandelier to shatter at my feet. I flung my arm over my face; bits of glass stung as they hit my skin, but I didn't feel the wet ooze of blood. Matty was screaming her head off somewhere in the background. I hoped she was okay. She had to be okay. Maybe the noise had scared her.

"So close," the golem hissed. I couldn't tell where her voice was coming from; somehow it seemed to be coming from all around me, like it was being carried on the wind. "You'll have no choice but to help me if you're hurt so bad you can't move . . ."

The hat rack Jed and Matty and I had laughed at what seemed like so long ago crashed over in front of me. The golem laughed cruelly somewhere in the background.

I needed time to think. But I couldn't stop to think or something would smash my head in. I wished I could call for a time-out. But this wasn't like a sports game. I wasn't even good at sports. So that was probably a good thing.

Something I couldn't see crashed just behind me with the splintering sound of broken glass. Jed and Matty screaming was a background noise at this point. I *had* to figure out what to do!

I kept running ahead . . . and hit a wall. Literally. For the first time, I'd made it to the very back of the garage.

There wasn't treasure back here after all.

I spun. On my right, a massive chest of drawers loomed over me. On my left, I could see the side wall peeking out through a cluster of old lamps. The only way to go was the way I'd come from.

Where Elsa was standing now. She took a step closer to me, her half-dirt face twisted into an expression of triumph. "There you are, Leah," she said, moving closer. Grains of dirt scattered behind her as she walked. "But you wanted me to find you the whole time, didn't you?"

"No," I said because obviously I didn't want to be crushed by a chandelier, but she only snorted. It sounded like a footstep crunching on gravel.

"You say that, but you forget that you created me as a reflection of you," she said. "All those things you were thinking about while you formed me—I saw them. I understood them."

"Then you understood them wrong," I said desperately. "I love Matty and Jed. I would never want to hurt them."

Elsa giggled. It sounded odd coming from her monstrous dirt face. "I understood everything right," she said. "Maybe I don't need to threaten your cousins or hurt you to make you do what I want. Maybe I can help you, and you can help me."

Help me? But . . .

"You don't like *yourself*," she continued. "And that feeling was in every other feeling you gave me. You hate your nose. You hate your family history. You hate how other people see you at school. So what's the solution for that?" Her worm-lips widened, her dull black stone eye glistening strangely. "Let me help you."

"No!" I cried. I wasn't sure if I was yelling in response to her offer of help or the thing about me not liking myself. Because she was definitely wrong about that second thing. Or . . . was she?

Zaide had talked about things we could and couldn't change. I couldn't change who I was. But I *could* change how I felt about it.

"Yessss," the golem hissed, stepping forward again. "I can get you back in with Isabella Lynch. I can help get you money so you can get that nose job."

And how I felt about it was . . . I didn't want to be

friends with Isabella Lynch anymore. I didn't want to be *like* Isabella Lynch anymore. I wanted to be friends with people who liked me for who I was.

"You're wrong," I said. "That's not what I want. No matter what my nose looks like. Not if it means being rotten on the inside."

Elsa just hissed as she came closer. Dirt crumbled from her chin. Was she losing even more of her humanity now? "You gave me how you feel. I know better than you, Leah." She gave me a ghoulish smile. "But fine. If you won't let me help you, I have no problem forcing you."

I took a step back but just hit the wall again. I'd given her my feelings. She wanted the same things I'd wanted, to fit in and be popular, only I hadn't treated her like she'd fit in. Shame flickered through me. I'd treated her like something not human—which, technically, she was—by ordering her around, making her hide herself when other people were nearby . . .

Maybe I could use this. "Elsa," I called. She scowled at me. "I understand how you feel. Like, exactly. I'm sorry for the way I treated you."

She furrowed her brows at me. One normal, one that looked to be made up of tiny pebbles of gravel.

"What you're missing is that people change," I continued. "I'm different from the way I was when I made you.
My feelings are different. Like I was just saying."

Her scowl was slipping away, replaced with a wormy
lip twisted in thought.

"Maybe we can be different together," I encouraged.
Though every cell of my body screamed to be farther
away from the golem, I took a step closer to her. Then
another. The screaming intensified, but I kept going.
"You don't have to work for Zaide anymore. We can be
friends together. Hang out. All of that stuff." The things
I wanted the Three Ds to say to me. Though they'd kind
of said all this, hadn't they? Just not so obviously. "I
don't want to be friends with Isabella Lynch anymore.
I don't need to be popular to be happy. And neither do
you. Come here. Give me a hug."

She moved until we were close enough to touch.
Close enough for her to reach out and plunge her fingers
into my chest and rip out my heart.

But she didn't.

She smiled, pleased. Those wormy lips of hers opened,
showing her teeth and a pink flash of tongue—

I dove at her, my right hand going straight for her
mouth. She shrieked. The non-dirt half of her mouth

snapped at me with sharp-looking teeth, but the other half didn't have sharp teeth to snap. So I jammed my fingers into the dirt half, trying to ignore how oozy and slimy the worm-lip felt.

My fingers closed around her tongue. It still felt fully tongue-ish, fat and wet and gross, though on the top of it I could feel the imprinted letters of the *shem*. I grimaced as it lashed in my grip, trying to escape. One of my teachers had told us once that the tongue was the strongest muscle in the body. I believed her now.

The golem suddenly stopped struggling. She stared up at me with pleading eyes. Well, eye. "Leah," she said, or tried to say. It came out more like *luh-uh*. "*Dun do thus.*" She clenched her fingers into a fist. Was she trying to use magic?

Something creaked horribly behind me. I closed my eyes. "I'm sorry," I said, and I pulled.

It happened so fast. Her tongue came free in my fingers, shriveling into a damp scrap of paper by the time I pulled it from her mouth. Her body crumbled into dirt.

Not fast enough, though, to stop the tower of lamps from falling on me.

CHAPTER TWENTY-ONE

I FELL HARD UNDER THE lamps, shielding my head from any shattering glass. My ankle twisted painfully beneath me, but I pushed the agony out of my mind as I struggled to stand. I had more important things than myself to worry about right now.

Getting Matty and Jed out took kind of a while, considering none of us really wanted to touch the sharp, rusted blades. Also, they both looked like they'd seen a ghost, their eyes wide and faces drained of all color. But eventually I managed to create a big enough opening for them to squeeze through and out, so all was well. Or as well as things could be, I guess.

Of course, the jagged pain coursing through my right ankle had me biting back a scream every time I limped on it, but I could deal with that later.

Later came after we rescued Uncle Marvin, Aunt Jessie, and my dad. I'd wondered why my dad hadn't come running inside after me while I was in there battling for my life, but our discovery explained it. He had indeed walked up to the door . . . and promptly collapsed into a deep sleep on the threshold. Aunt Jessie and Uncle Marvin were inside snoozing on the couch. More golem magic, apparently. We were panicked a little at first, but all we had to do was shake them and scream into their faces, and they woke right up, groggy and bewildered but otherwise okay.

They said there must have been some kind of gas leak that made them pass out and that we had to get out now, now, now, and they'd call 911. They did ask a lot of questions about the mess in the garage that they'd glimpsed through the open door, which dropped off as soon as I tried to limp down the stairs and stopped biting back that scream. Then everybody except Aunt Jessie—who stayed to direct the firemen—piled into our car and drove right to the hospital. I was on a different floor from Zaide as they put a brace on my ankle. I pretended to be too dopey on pain meds to answer any questions, and then suddenly I blinked and I was at home. In my bed. Alone.

It was actually kind of a relief—that Jed and Matty weren't there. I didn't really feel like answering their questions just then. I knew that they deserved answers after all they'd been through, but surely they could wait until I was feeling—

"Is she up?" My door banged open, slamming into the wall with a crash.

Well. If I hadn't been up before, I certainly would be now.

Jed and Matty filed into my room, closing the door behind them, gently this time. "Hey, guys," I said feebly, dropping my head back onto my pillow like it was too heavy to hold up. "I'm kind of . . . tired . . ."

"Not too tired to talk to us," Matty said firmly. She grabbed my desk chair and dragged it over beside my bed, taking a seat. Jed stood next to her, resting his hand on the back of the chair.

Both stared at me grimly. I waited for them to start talking, but they just kept staring.

I couldn't take the uncomfortable silence. "What do you want to talk about?" I asked them.

Matty's eyes nearly bulged out of her head. "Are you *seriously* asking me that right now?"

"Asking *us* that," Jed corrected. This would usually be the time when he'd make a joke or something to break the tension, but this was evidently too serious a moment.

I sighed. "I can tell you what happened, but you're not going to believe me."

This made Jed snort a laugh. "I'm pretty sure our minds are open right now. After what we just experienced and all."

I sighed again. Tried to sigh as long and loud as I could, to demonstrate how much I was suffering not only with this badly sprained ankle but with the emotional pain they were inflicting upon me, but they seemed unmoved. So I told them. I told them everything. I bared all, down to what I was feeling and thinking. From me worrying about Zaide and how everything would change, to Zaide telling me the story about the golem, to me finding the envelope of dirt and the *shem*. To me mixing up the golem in the soup pot and trying to disguise her as a friend. To everything that ensued.

"So I think this is an example of something he said

that can't be fixed," I said mournfully. "No more chess with Zaide. You guys will keep on getting awards in soccer and baseball and going to your school far away, and we'll never see each other."

"You forgot to mention that I'm going to fail math class," Jed said.

My eyes narrowed. "Don't even joke about that."

Jed thumped down on the bed beside me. "But that's all I do well."

Despite myself, a tiny smile twitched at my lips. "That's not true."

"Right," Matty chimed in. "You also beat people up."

"That too," he bragged, and now we were all more relaxed. Which might have been the whole point, I realized, of him making a joke.

"Anyway," Matty said. "Leah, why did you think it was a good idea to build that thing in the first place?"

The words stuck in my throat. I had to clear it to get them to come out. "Zaide needed someone to look after him." My voice was tiny. "He needed help."

Matty rolled her eyes. "Not buying it."

I got defensive. "But that's why—"

"There has to be more to it." Matty talked over me.

"Or else you would have ended it when you realized she was doing a *terrible* job."

She knew me too well. Usually I liked it, but now it made me want to cry. "I didn't want to lose you guys, either." If I kept my voice as tiny as possible, maybe no tears would fall. "I didn't want our Saturdays to end."

That left the room quiet. Matty stared at me. Jed stared at me.

And then Matty sighed. "We don't want to lose any of that, either," she said. "You know, I realized in the garage as those rusty blades were spinning toward our faces . . . we'd kind of been pretending that this all wasn't happening. That Zaide wasn't . . . wasn't . . ." Her voice trembled, and she looked down. Which made me realize: She hadn't been in denial because she didn't care. She'd been in denial because she cared too much. Which, somehow, made it all easier for me to deal with.

She cleared her throat and looked up. "I don't know what's going to happen," she said. "We're getting older. Of course things are going to change. But . . . at least we can go through it all together."

She grabbed my hand and squeezed. I squeezed

back. It was me trying to say all the things I suddenly couldn't say because my throat had swelled up with tears.

"Like Matty said, things are going to change," Jed added. I waited for the punch line, but his voice was dead serious. "But not the most important things. Whether we see each other every Saturday or not, we'll always be cousins. We'll always be friends. That's something we *can* make sure of."

He was right. Even if we didn't have our Saturday afternoons anymore, we could still make an effort. We could still stay friends. We'd all have to try harder, but to throw back to my conversation with Zaide, it was something we could fix.

Jed cleared his throat. "And I've already talked to my math teacher about getting a tutor at school," he said. "Zaide said he was proud of me."

And also . . . maybe at school, I could change if I stopped trying so hard to keep everything the same. Change could be okay. And maybe acting like I cared about myself, like I thought I was worthy of being liked, was the first step toward changing the thoughts in my head.

Matty smiled at me. "He's right. I'm in."

I knew what I had to do. It would hurt to say it, but she was right. I had to try. "Me too," I said. "Matilda."

We hung out for a while, shooting the breeze. I'd always liked that expression, just because it struck me as so impossible. You couldn't actually shoot the breeze. You'd probably kill someone trying.

My parents interrupted us with a knock on the door. "Matilda, Jed, your parents are ready to leave," Mom said softly. Matty—Matilda—and Jed gave me air-kisses and left, their feet stomping down the stairs. I expected my parents to follow them, but they only stepped inside.

Ambush! I couldn't even run away.

"I'm so tired," I said feebly. "And my poor ankle hurts soooo much."

"Nice try," my dad said. "Leah, we need to talk to you."

I wanted to sigh, but it was suddenly like I couldn't take in any air. Because I knew what they wanted to talk to me about.

Mom sat down on the edge of my bed. She was hanging most of the way off, so she couldn't have been very comfortable. My dad stood beside her, resting a hand on her shoulder. "Leah, all of the necessary documents have been signed and agreed upon. Zaide will be moving from the hospital to an assisted-living facility." Her lips twitched in a sad smile. "Nobody's happy about this, but we *are* relieved. They're going to take much better care of him there than we would be able to out here."

I stared at the ceiling. I wasn't going to cry. I wasn't.

Even if everything was over. My plans had failed. Zaide was leaving his house behind.

"We have some pictures of his new room if you'd like to see them," Dad continued. "Here. Check them out."

If I spoke, I would cry. So I let him swipe through the pictures on his phone in front of my face. The rooms he showed me looked pretty similar to a hotel. More like a hotel than a hospital, actually. They even had a pool.

"See?" Dad withdrew his phone. "Not so bad, right?"

"And we'll still be visiting him every Saturday afternoon. Your cousins, too," Mom said.

"But what about Zaide?" I asked. "He didn't want to go."

Mom shook her head. "It's funny. He totally changed his mind after you had those ten minutes with him," she said. "You must have said something that made him realize he couldn't live on his own with a broken hip."

Or . . . he was learning to accept the things he couldn't change. To make the best of them.

We would still have our Saturday afternoons. Even if they were a little bit different. And I would keep playing chess with Zaide. I would keep loving Zaide. Lots of other things might change, but that wouldn't. I wouldn't let it.

"We'll go see him tomorrow?" I asked.

My mom leaned over and kissed me atop my head. In the very place Isabella Lynch had massaged looking for horns. "Of course."

I took a deep breath. "Fine." It would be hard. I would have to accept it. And make the best of it. Because things couldn't go back to the way they were, and I hated that, but I couldn't make it different.

My head itched thinking about where Isabella Lynch had touched it. Maybe *that* I could make different. But not by changing how I felt toward Isabella Lynch. I had to work on the feelings I had toward myself.

My mind began to race. I had a lot to plan before going back.

CHAPTER
TWENTY-TWO

I MIGHT NOT HAVE BEEN able to change anything with Zaide, but I *could* change what happened in school. Maybe not uproot thousands of years of everybody hating on the Jews, or even change Isabella Lynch's mind. But I could change how they were treating me and how I reacted to it. And maybe also how I treated other people.

So come lunch the next day, I didn't hide in the second-floor bathroom. For one thing, I couldn't climb the stairs on crutches with my ankle in a brace and carry all my stuff at the same time. But that wasn't the real reason. I was actually glad for my crutches and my ankle. I had to focus hard to get anywhere, and all that focus and work kept me from totally freaking out as I approached Isabella's table.

It took a long time for me to get anywhere, so it gave them plenty of time to stare and whisper. Enough time for a cold sweat to break out on the back of my neck and for me to begin quaking on the inside.

I stopped at the head of their table. Even though the golem was gone, hopefully forever, they'd left her usual seat open. Isabella was staring at me like I was something gross she'd stepped in. "Do you want something?" Her voice was syrupy sweet, of course.

I took a deep breath. "I wanted to let you know that Jews do not control the media. Or the government. I kind of wish we did." I let out a deranged sort of laugh. "It would make my life a whole lot easier. No more homework ever, am I right? But no, we don't. So no, Isabella, I can't help you become president."

Her face fell, but only a little. She managed to hold most of it up in an expression of cautious optimism. "I didn't think that," she said. "Of course not. That's ridiculous."

Everybody was staring at us. I cleared my throat so I could speak as loudly as possible. "Also, I wanted to show you that I don't have horns." I leaned my head over the table, letting my hair touch the sticky surface. It was gross, but I persisted long enough to run my fingers through it, parting the strands and exposing enough of my head that it was very clear nothing was growing there but hair. "I'm just a person. Like you. With hair on my head. And ears. And nothing else."

When I raised my head back up, Isabella's face was startlingly white. White enough that I'd be worried a vampire had snuck in and drained her of blood if I hadn't known better. Her throat kept working like she was trying to swallow. Her friends were glancing in her direction, as if they were trying to meet her eye, but she had eyes only for me. "Ridiculous," she said, but the lightness in her voice sounded so forced I surely couldn't be the only one who heard it. "Of course you don't have horns."

I wrinkled my brows in mock confusion. "You seem really sure for someone who made fun of me for being Jewish when I went over to your house. Remember how you mocked me for being selfish and for being greedy?

Even though I'm not either of those things? And how you called me a monster? Yeah, you definitely said that. It's seared into my brain. I couldn't forget it if I wanted to."

"Ridiculous," Isabella said again, but she sounded way less sure. She cast a look around the table. Some of her friends nodded at her, like, *How dare this girl accuse you of such things*, but others were staring down at the table, or chewing on the insides of their cheeks as they looked at me.

I lifted my chin up high. Part of me was shriveling inside from all the attention on me—the tables next door were quiet now, too, listening—but another part was basking in it. It was weird and contradictory, and I wasn't sure I liked it. It wasn't fair that I had to deal with this. With people hating me. But sometimes you had to do things you didn't like and learn to deal with it. That was life. "I don't want anything to do with you."

I turned to go before she could react. But turning for me now took ages, so I could easily hear her hurl at my back, "Good because I don't want anything to do with you, either."

I took a halting step. Maybe nothing would change. And then I heard a hesitant voice say, "You know, like, my stepdad is Jewish, Isabella."

I couldn't hear any more. A fire invigorated my steps. I swung myself over to the table in the back where the Three Ds still sat. They were staring at me, too, as I approached.

I stopped at the edge of their table. As much as I wanted to swing myself into my usual seat and pretend that nothing was wrong, I knew I had to talk to them. Also, Dallas had piled her books and stuff on my seat, just in case I didn't get the hint.

"Hi," I said, staring down at the table between us. For some reason, this seemed much harder than confronting Isabella Lynch. I didn't care anymore if Isabella liked me or not, but I realized that I wanted the Three Ds to like me—despite my nose, despite the fact that I had been a pretty crappy friend. "You should know that I'm really awkward. I've wanted to be your friend all year, but I didn't think you wanted to be mine. I guess I'm bad at reading cues." I glanced up, afraid they were sharing a *look* over my head. But they weren't. "I was so busy worrying about my old friends and trying to keep in touch with them that I didn't think to make time for new friends. I guess . . . I wanted to be popular because I thought being popular would mean having friends no matter what, but I was wrong. Really wrong. I'm sorry I was a jerk. I want to try again if you'll let me."

I held my breath. Deanna, Dallas, and Daisy stared blankly at me. Maybe they hadn't heard anything I'd said? I *had* talked kind of fast. Maybe I should say it all over again. Maybe I should start with the apology this time. *I'm sorry, you guys. I want to be your friend.* No, that came off as too desperate.

A loud *thump* broke me out of my thoughts. Dallas had lifted her books off my seat and deposited them onto the table. I raised my eyebrows at her. She gestured to my spot.

My heart hovered high in my chest. I limped over to my seat and managed to slide myself in, leaning my crutches against the table. "Thanks," I said.

Daisy didn't so much as bat an eyelash at me. "So you have to tell us what Isabella's house looked like," she said. "Is she actually as rich as she says?"

Just like that? I took another deep breath. She was looking beyond my nose. She *wanted* to be my friend. Or was she not so much looking beyond my nose as not looking at it at all?

Had I been using my nose as an excuse?

I could mull that over later. "I hate to say it, but it was a really nice house," I said. "She's still a rotten person, though."

"Right?" Deanna propped her chin up on her hands. "You know, we used to be friends when we were little. She's pretty racist. I should have warned you."

I gave her a tiny smile. She gave me one back. I took a deep breath. "Remember what you said about starting a chess club?" I asked. She nodded, her eyes lighting up. "Well, I'm in."

Daisy and Dallas groaned good-naturedly as Deanna clapped her hands. "Yessss!" she cheered. "I'm thinking Wednesdays after school? We can ask Ms. Bunce to advise. And I was thinking we'd do outreach to the fifth-grade girls, like in their math classes . . ."

Our conversation made me feel warm. Or not so much warm but as though I had been frozen and was beginning to thaw in the sun. Because it wasn't like one conversation could fix everything, but it felt good. It felt like I was moving in the right direction.

Even if my nose wasn't really standing in my way (literally or figuratively), I still didn't love it. This wasn't a movie where I'd have a sudden change of heart and swoon into the mirror, magically in love with this feature I had cursed my whole life.

But maybe I wouldn't get a nose job the second I turned eighteen. Maybe I'd give it a little time. Maybe I was growing into it.

AUTHOR'S NOTE

The golem is a well-known figure in Jewish mythology. There are a number of different stories and different interpretations of the golem, but for the most part, they involve a member of the Jewish community sculpting a figure out of clay for protection against those who wish to do the community harm. In some tales, the golem is unable to speak (which would have been a serious bummer for Elsa). In others, the letters of creation weren't written on a paper and inserted into the golem's mouth, but written on their forehead or hung around their neck. The most famous tale of the golem is *The Golem of Prague*, which was the foundation for the golems in this book—but I was inspired by pieces of the earlier tales as well. If you're interested in reading more about the golem, I encourage you to seek out all of these different and equally fascinating legends!

So much of Zaide's character was inspired by my real-life Zaide, Sidney Nevins: climbing onto the roof of his old telephone company building in his nineties; his love of chess; and, sadly, his battle with Alzheimer's disease. While my real-life Zaide had a very different personality from book Zaide, I have to say thank you to him and Bubbe for being the inspiration for this book.

Like Leah, I spent most of my Saturday afternoons growing up at Zaide's house with my extended family, horsing around with my cousins and sitting around the kitchen table scribbling in various fancy notebooks. Thank you to Grandma Roz, who I so wish was here to see this book, Uncle Sol and Aunt Debbi, Uncle Darryl and Aunt Susan, Dave, Dan, and Rachel, Cousins Marcia, Bill, Michelle, and Brandon, my parents and siblings, and my own faraway cousins. Special thanks to Dan and Rachel for being my Jed and Matty. Thank you all for being the heart.

It was a long, twisty, difficult road to get to this book. Thank you to my agent, Merrilee Heifetz, who stuck with me the whole way through and didn't let me crash, along with assistant extraordinaire Rebecca Eskildsen and the rest of the team at Writers House.

I'm so grateful to my publishing team at Roaring Brook Press for making this book the best book it could be. Thank you to my editors, Jen Besser and Mekisha Telfer, for *getting* Leah and this book, and all of the work you did to make it better. Olivia Chin Mueller, I can't get over how gorgeous and perfect your cover illustration is, and Cassie Gonzales, same for your book design. Thank you also to Brian Luster, Allyson Floridia, John Nora, and Morgan Kane.

And thank you to Jeremy Bohrer, for everything.